SWEET CHRISTMAS KISSES SERIES

# Cabin Fever
## WITH MY
# First Flame

**MADISON LOVE**

Copyright © October 2024 by Madison Love

All rights reserved.

No part of this publication may be reproduced, distributed, or transmitted in any form or by any means, including photocopying, recording, or other electronic or mechanical methods, without the prior written permission of the publisher, except as permitted by U.S. copyright law. For permission requests, contact

3n1publishing@gmail.com or madison@madisonloveromance.com

The story, all names, characters, and incidents portrayed in this production are fictitious. No identification with actual persons (living or deceased), places, buildings, and products is intended or should be inferred.

All Bible references are from the English Standard Version (ESV) unless otherwise noted.

# Contents

1. Bailey — 1
2. Finn — 12
3. Bailey — 21
4. Finn — 30
5. Bailey — 39
6. Finn — 48
7. Bailey — 57
8. Finn — 65
9. Bailey — 75
10. Finn — 83
11. Bailey — 92
12. Finn — 101

| | | |
|---|---|---|
| 13. | Bailey | 111 |
| 14. | Finn | 120 |
| 15. | Bailey | 129 |
| 16. | Finn | 139 |
| 17. | Bailey | 152 |
| 18. | Finn | 160 |
| 19. | Bailey | 170 |
| 20. | Finn | 179 |
| 21. | Bailey | 187 |
| 22. | Finn | 198 |
| Epilogue | | 210 |
| The Sweet Christmas Series | | 217 |
| Coming Soon! | | 221 |
| Blurb | | 223 |
| Excerpt from The Beanbaggers of Cornhole County | | 225 |
| Also By Madison Love | | 233 |

## Chapter One

### Bailey

"Mom, if I have to listen to one more Christmas song on this trip, I'm going to pull out my hair and end up looking like Uncle Baxter," my oldest daughter, Ella, says dramatically as she reaches for the radio controls to change the channel. I'll be the first to admit that my brother, Baxter, is a bit thin on top, but he's a far cry from being bald.

I smack her hand away and give my 14-year-old the stink eye, refusing to listen to K-pop or another Disney actress-turned-pop star. "As pilot of this ship, radio controls belong to me, Miss Thang. When you have your own car, you can play whatever you want. Besides, Christmas music is the 'bomb diggity,' and I get to listen to it for only one month out of the year."

Ella folds her arms across her chest, staring out the window and watching the snow that is starting to fall in earnest now. It's coming down heavy enough that I'm becoming concerned. "Don't pretend that you haven't been listening to it since July, Mom. And what is 'bomb diggity,' anyway? Who talks like that?"

We're driving on a winding backroad that leads into my hometown of Lake George, New York—a small tourist village that boasts picturesque views and amazing skiing this time of year. It also boasts two-lane highways butted up against a mountain with blind curves and a cliff. I grimace as the lines in the road start slowly disappearing under a blanket of white fluff and use my daughter's question as a distraction from my fraying nerves. The last thing I need is for Ella to see me panic.

"Oh, forgive me. You kids say, 'It's slay,' now. How could I forget?" My sarcasm doesn't go unnoticed by Ella, who is the spitting image of me when I was a teenager. She has the same long, blond hair and large, blue eyes that stare back at me every day, but the similarities don't stop there.

Ella also has my spit-fire personality and a mouth that gets her in trouble—like right now.

She turns her head slowly in my direction and leans away from me, a slow smile forming on her lips. "Because you're *old*."

"I'm 35! That's not old!" I retort, falling into her trap. Ella takes great pride in trying to get a reaction from me, and I hate to say it, but she succeeds more often than she fails.

"Well, you drive like you're old. At this rate, I can get out and walk to Nana's faster. Want me to drive?" Ella asks hopefully.

I bark out a laugh that Ella doesn't find amusing in the slightest. "You're 14 and have two more years before you can drive. No, Sweetheart, you get to be my passenger princess for a little while longer." I glance over my shoulder at my other two princesses, Ava and Mia, who are sleeping soundly in the jump seats of my food truck.

"Dad would let me drive. He's done it before," Ella says with her lower lip turned out. She's trying to pit me against her father, but that's one trap I don't fall for. I may not be *in* love with Daniel anymore, but I'll never say a bad word about him to our kids. It doesn't matter that he cheated on me, sold our restaurant, and ran away with the hostess. His relationship with our daughters is between him and them, and his actions will speak for themselves. I'll be there to help pick up the pieces when he inevitably breaks our daughters' hearts, even if I pray every day that's not what happens.

I grip the steering wheel almost to the point where my knuckles are as white as the ground outside. "Ella, when you visit your dad for the summer, then you can ask him to let you drive. I'll even promise to give you some driving lessons when the snow melts. But now is not the time. We're in the middle of the snowstorm that wasn't supposed to hit until tomorrow, and I can barely see the road."

Ella senses the tension in my voice and knows that it's time to hold back on the snark. She's quiet for a long time, which basically means she lasts until the end of "It's the Most Wonderful Time of the Year" by Andy Williams. Four minutes must feel like forever for a teenage girl with a lot on her mind.

"Mom, do you think that you'll ever get married again?" Ella asks hesitantly. "Or do you believe that true love only comes around once?"

My poor baby left behind her first and only boyfriend back in Myrtle Beach, along with all of her friends. She's feeling the loss of them as much as she is the loss of her father. I reach over as far as my seatbelt will let me and hold out my hand. Instead of joining our palms together, she gives me a 'low five' and then points toward the road.

Returning my eyes so that they're focused out the front window, I tell her, "Yes, Ella, I believe that true love comes around more than once. Believe it or not, I've loved two men in my life. As for getting married again, I honestly don't know. If love finds me a third time, I'm open to it. If it doesn't, I'm okay with that, too."

"Is Finn the guy you loved before Dad?" Ella asks, throwing me completely off guard. I can't remember a single time that I've ever mentioned Finn since he left me back in high school, and I know for a fact I never brought up his name around the girls.

"Uh. Um. How do you know about Finn? Did your father say something to you?" My parents wouldn't have said anything because they know that Finn Hollister is a topic that was always off-limits in our household. As once my high school sweetheart and Daniel's best friend, Finn didn't just leave me. He left us both.

She shakes her head, but then nods. "Dad didn't say anything to me directly. I overheard him talking on the phone with his friend, Bryce. He told Bryce to keep you away from Finn since your paths are bound to cross."

"What? Why would he..." I'm interrupted by a slight rumble in the truck and a lurching motion that warrants my full attention. I glance down at the gas gauge, which is still showing half a tank. I frown. It's in the same position as when we passed through Albany a few hours back, and I can't help but wonder how long it's been stuck.

"Is everything okay?" Ella asks worriedly.

"Maybe," I say, tapping the glass on my dashboard. "The gas gauge is stuck, and I don't know how long it's been like that. We're seven miles from Pop's and Nana's place, so if I can make it to the top of the hill, we can coast down the other side, right into town," I say, spewing my thoughts out loud.

"We should have filled up in Albany," my daughter says unhelpfully.

She's not wrong. Regardless, I didn't have enough cash left to purchase a full tank and the credit cards are maxed. Prior to the divorce, Daniel sold our restaurant and paid off the mortgage on the house. His plan was to offer me the food truck in exchange for him getting to keep our home. Thankfully, the truck was in my parents' name, and the judge mandated that either the house be sold or that Daniel buys me out. With the sale still pending, I'll have to wait for my half.

After the final turn, I can see the crest of the hill up ahead. I channel my "Little Engine Who Could" and mutter out a chant, "I think I can. I think I can. I think I can." When the truck sputters and comes to a stop less than 50 feet from the top, I bang my forehead against the steering wheel. "I guess I can't."

Refusing to go into full-blown panic mode, I pull out my phone and check to see if I have any bars in the right-hand corner. Reception in the Adirondack mountains is spotty at best, but with heavy snowfall and ominous clouds overhead, it would be a miracle if I could even get a text through. The "SOS" is prominently displayed where the stair-stepping bars should be, so I hold the side and volume buttons to access emergency services. The call doesn't go through, and I'm forced to use the satellite feature to get routed.

When the dispatcher answers, I explain the situation and give her my location. I also inform her that I have three children with me, hoping to be bumped up on the priority list. She reassures me that help is on the way, but it could take up to a few hours. "Sit tight, and don't venture out. There's a blizzard passing through the area, and it is expected to drop seven to ten feet of snow," the friendly dispatcher tells me.

When I hang up the phone, Ella gazes at me with frightened eyes. "It's going to be all right, Sweetheart," I say, unbuckling and pulling her into a motherly embrace. "Snow in this area is not uncommon, and people need to be rescued all the time. We have sleeping bags in the back to stay warm, plenty of food and water, and the new cold-weather gear Nana sent you girls for this trip. Let's be grateful to God we have shelter in this storm."

Ella nods. Mia and Ava both wake up now that the vehicle has come to a stop and the temperatures inside are slowly dropping. It's no surprise that both girls have to pee, so I dig around in the back of the truck through our belongings to find a bucket. While Mia is on the makeshift potty, Ella asks more about Finn.

"Why did you and Finn break up in high school?" Ella asks.

"It's a long story, Ella. Maybe another time," I reply, darting my eyes between Ava and Mia.

She waves her hand toward the front window where the snow is well over a foot deep, and a plow has yet to come by. "It's not like we're going anywhere, and we have the time."

I sigh. "It's not that big of a deal, Ella. Finn was a year older than me and a grade ahead. When he graduated, he went to Buffalo to train as a firefighter. He was supposed to be gone for six months and then come back for me. Our plan was to get married when I graduated. I waited for him, but six months turned into a year, and there was no sign of Finn. The calls slowly stopped coming until I received a letter in the mail saying he was moving to California to fight the wildfires—without me."

My six-year-old daughter, Ava, comes over and sits in my lap, asking where we are. I tell her that we ran out of gas and that there are knights in shining armor coming to rescue us. Ava giggles, but ten-year-old Mia is less enthusiastic about our impromptu camping trip. Pulling up her pants, she comes over and sits crisscross on the floor next to Ella. "What happened next? Is that when you fell in love with Dad?"

I nod. "With Finn, I loved him from the moment he moved to town my freshman year. Our chemistry was off the charts, and we were inseparable for those three years before he left. Your dad was his best friend, and the three of us always hung out together. So, when Finn never came back, the friendship between your dad and I grew into something more. We dated for a couple of years, fell in love, and then got married."

Ella's eyes twinkle with mischief. "So, Finn was the hot firefighter who burned you, and Dad was the rebound guy. Any regrets about not chasing after Finn after everything that has happened between you and Dad?"

I narrow my eyes at Ella. "I can always count on you to call it like you see it, Ella. However, I wouldn't have put it quite that way. I loved your father very much. I never saw your father as a rebound, and our relationship took time to develop. My love for Finn was instant and intense. My love for your father grew from friendship. I loved them differently, but no less than with all my heart. I have no regrets, especially since God gave me the three of you. I wouldn't change a thing."

We have a group hug before Ella sits back on her haunches. "Do you think you might run into Finn? How cool would that be to get a second chance?"

I shake my head adamantly. "Finn lives in California, Sweetie. There's not a chance..."

*Ahh!* My girls scream in unison when a man in a black ski mask begins pounding on the window, but I can't get a good look at him from my position. "We're here to rescue you, miladies. We got a call that you were in need of assistance."

Three more sets of eyes hidden behind neon-colored ski masks peer at us from over the hood of the truck. The person wearing the bright yellow ski mask rolls his eyes. I can't see his face, but I get the feeling he can't be older than 15 or 16. He waves us over and then points to two quad runners that each seat four people. "We're your ride. Grab your stuff, and let's go."

I give him a grateful smile and then make sure each of the girls are bundled up in their new coats, boots, scarves, hats, and gloves. They each have a backpack with a few changes of clothes and basic toiletries. The wind is picking up, and the visibility is getting closer to zero with every passing second.

I wrap a scarf around my face before opening the door and falling knee-deep in fresh powder. The man doesn't bother to look at me as he hastily helps each of the girls and gets them settled into the back of the quad runners. When he comes back to give me an assist, he stops in his tracks, and his eyes widen in surprise.

I turn around to see what has caught his attention, wondering if there is a bear behind me. When I see nothing, I shrug and move past him, taking the last available seat in the ATV. When he hops into the driver's seat, I tap him on the shoulder and give him the address that we're staying at in town.

"No can do," he replies. "Visibility will be zero within the next ten minutes, and it's too dangerous to stay out here in the middle of a blizzard. Our cabin is on the other side of the hill, less than a mile away. You and your girls will be safe with us while we ride out the storm. Don't worry, Bailey Bug. You're in good hands."

*Bailey Bug*? Only one person has ever called me that.

"Finn?"

# Chapter Two

## Finn

FIGHTING FIRES AND JUMPING from an airplane is easier than getting three boys to put down their game controllers to help me bring in extra firewood. After a few grumbles, Micah—the oldest of the three—is the first to relent and do the right thing. Since the eight-year-old twins, Jonah and Isaac, look up to their older brother, they quickly follow his lead.

"Let's gear up and move out," I tell them. "The sooner we get this done, the sooner you can get back to playing your game. And don't forget, the three of you need to help me decorate the inside of the cabin for Christmas this evening."

Micah nods and fights back his tears. At 16, he feels that it's his duty to be a rock for his brothers. "Mom always loved decorating for the holidays. She had the tree up before Thanksgiving, and our house always looked like it threw up Christmas. She always roped us into making cookies and singing carols. I didn't appreciate it then, but I'd give anything to be making gingerbread men with her right now."

Since Micah isn't a hugger, I pat him on the back. "I'm not much of a baker, but we can try to make some cookies tonight if you want. Who knows? It might be fun."

Micah shakes his head and helps his younger brothers get dressed. "It was always Mom's thing. You don't have to try and replace her, Finn. We'll create our own traditions now that we live with you."

The four of us spend the next hour hauling wood from the shed at the edge of the property, loading up the quad ATVs with as much as they can hold. We're in the process of unloading the last of the firewood when the walkie-talkie on my hip bursts with static followed by the fire chief's clipped tone.

"Hollister, are you there? Come in, Hollister."

I motion for the boys to stand on the porch and out of the weather, then press the talk button to reply. "This is Hollister. What's up, Chief?"

"We have an emergency. There is a woman and her three children stuck in the storm not far from your location. The plows can't keep up with the roads in town, let alone clear the highway. This storm is turning into a full-on blizzard, and you're the only one close enough to help them," he says.

I turn to face three boys who have the Hollister gene coursing through their veins. "Micah, I'll need your assistance to drive the other ATV. Ugh! I can't leave your brothers here alone."

"We can help!" Jonah shouts, puffing out his chest.

"We can be brave, just like you!" Isaac adds.

I smile proudly at the three boys, who are practically bouncing on their toes, ready to jump into action. "Are you sure? It could be dangerous."

Three heads of black hair bob in unison, their dark brown eyes gleaming with excitement. I press the talk button again. "Chief, let dispatch know that help is on the way."

"Roger. Thanks, Finn. I know you're taking some time off to spend with the boys and grieving the loss of…"

"It's fine. We're happy to help," I reply, cutting him off. The holidays are going to be hard enough without the reminder that Jenny won't be here with us.

After receiving the approximate location of the stranded family, we set off with Isaac as my copilot while Jonah rides with Micah. The highway isn't far from us, about a mile away and on the other side of the mountain.

"Who would be stupid enough to drive in this weather and then run out of gas?" Isaac asks, having overhead the details that the Chief relayed to us.

"We don't call people 'stupid,' Isaac. Accidents happen all the time." I chastise. "In all fairness, the storm wasn't supposed to hit until tomorrow and is going to be much worse than expected."

When we crest the hill, the stranded vehicle comes into view. The snow is nearly two feet deep, with six inches covering the roof and hood of a food truck. The visibility is getting worse, and there isn't much time to waste before it will be eight people stranded instead of four.

I don't see anyone in the driver's seat, so I peer inside the window and knock on the glass.

The three girls I can make out through the frosted window all scream when they see me. I chuckle since I can only imagine how a man in a black ski mask must look to them. "We're here to rescue you, miladies. We got a call that you were in need of assistance."

Micah stands on the front bumper as Isaac and Jonah climb onto the hood. Micah rolls his eyes at my attempt to put the girls at ease. He waves the girls over and then points to the ATVs parked at the top of the hill. "We're your ride. Grab your stuff, and let's go."

I'm grateful that the mom doesn't waste any time getting her kids squared away. She opens the door and jumps down, falling knee-deep in the snow. Quickly getting her feet under her, she turns toward her daughters. One by one, I help each of them down and pass them off to Micah. We get them situated in the quad runners before I return to help their mom.

The scarf covering the woman's face falls, and the plump pink lips that I used to nip at on a daily basis curve upward. I stop in my tracks as I take in the beautiful sight of Bailey McNamara, now Bailey Johnson. I frown; the name Johnson feels like acid in the pit of my stomach.

Bailey turns around to see what has captivated my attention, not realizing that it's her. She gives a quick shrug of her shoulders and then blows past me toward the ATVs. Once she's situated, I hop in the driver's seat only to feel a tap on my shoulder. She gives me her parent's address, but I shake my head.

"No can do. Visibility will be zero within the next ten minutes, and it's too dangerous to stay out here in the middle of a blizzard. Our cabin is on the other side of the hill, less than a mile away. You and your girls will be safe with us while we ride out the storm. Don't worry, Bailey Bug. You're in good hands."

Bailey's face contorts in confusion and then turns to mild disgust. "Finn?"

"In the flesh. I bet you thought you would never see me again?" I joke.

She doesn't laugh. Instead, she mutters, "Hoped was more like it. What are you doing here? Aren't you supposed to be in California jumping out of airplanes and fighting forest fires?"

"I've been back for three months. I live here now with Micah, Isaac, and Jonah," I tell her.

Isaac turns around in his seat to peer at Bailey. "When our mom died, Finn took us in but said 'he needed all the help he could get.' He moved us here because our Grandma and Grandpa live down the hill."

Micah tears off ahead of us, most likely showing off for the pretty little blond in his back seat. I try not to laugh but fail miserably. He's a Hollister to his core.

Bailey taps me on the shoulder again and leans forward so that her head is between Isaac and me. Her warm breath crystallizes in the air as she huffs. "Finn, we can't stay with you. Please take us to my parents' house."

"Bailey Bug..."

"It's Bailey. No 'Bug,'" she corrects. "You lost the right to call me that when you left and never came back."

"Why would I come back after....You know what? It doesn't matter. We'll leave the past where it belongs. Regardless, you're stuck with us until the storm passes. It's either that or you spend the next few days in your truck. Take it or leave it."

Her eyes widen as big as saucers as she screeches, "A few days?"

I bark out another laugh, this one without any mirth. "Haven't you heard? This storm is supposed to drop several feet of snow, and another one is right on its tail. When we get to the cabin, you can call Daniel and your parents and tell them that you're safe and 'snug as a *bug* in a rug.'"

"We don't live with Daddy anymore," says the little girl sitting next to Bailey. "He's getting married on Christmas to some hoochie-mama."

Bailey covers her daughter's mouth. "Ava, we don't call people 'hoochie-mama.' It's not very nice."

"But that's what you said to Nana," Ava replies, outing her mother. I doubt that Bailey had intended that particular conversation to be overheard, especially by tiny ears.

Bailey hugs her daughter apologetically. "I shouldn't have, Sweetie. That was wrong of me. Delaney is, um, a very nice woman who will make your father very happy."

The rest of the ride is ridden in silence as I think about the fact that Bailey is now single. I was the one who was supposed to make her happy, but I wasn't gone even three months before I found out she chose my best friend over me. Bailey promised she'd wait for me, but it didn't take long before she changed her mind.

As we pull up to the cabin, I force back the scowl that's threatening to emerge. The colorful Christmas lights twinkle brightly and mock me, reminding me that this is the season for forgiveness and letting go of old hurts. I forgave Daniel and Bailey a long time ago, but seeing her again is like opening up a fresh wound.

"We should get inside," I choke out as Micah and Jonah help their two passengers through the deep snow and onto the front porch. The stairs are barely discernable and are nearly covered under a blanket of white powder.

When Bailey and I make it to the front door, she sets down Ava and ushers her inside, leaving the two of us alone. She turns to me. "Thank you for rescuing us and providing a warm place for us to take shelter, Finn. We'll try to stay out of your way as much as we can, but we'll also do our part. We don't want to be a burden, so put us to work. We have no problem earning our keep."

I want to reach up and wipe the sadness from her eyes, but it hasn't been my place to do so in 18 years. "It's not a problem, and I'm glad we could help. As far as earning your keep, I don't suppose you know how to cook now. I remember that you used to burn nearly everything."

She giggles, the same tinkling sound that I remember. "Finn, I own a food truck and had a restaurant until a few months ago. I certainly hope that cooking is a skill I possess. If not, then I've disappointed more than half of Myrtle Beach and thousands of tourists."

I smile wanly and place my hand on the small of her back, guiding her inside. If Bailey has ever disappointed anyone, it was me when she broke my heart. I look up toward the heavens and wonder if God is playing a joke on me or if this is Him giving us the gift of a second chance.

## Chapter Three

### Bailey

The touch of Finn's hand on my back sends shivers down my spine and awakens the long-dormant butterflies in my stomach. I haven't felt them flutter around in years and don't know what to make of the sensation. I take a step away from Finn and help Ava get her boots off, placing them by the front door so that melted snow doesn't drip everywhere.

"This is a lovely home, Finn," I tell him, taking in the rustic charm of the cabin. The floors are made of polished wood, and the walls are a warm cream color. There aren't any pictures, and the place is devoid of any holiday decorations. "Your family always went all out during the holidays. I guess I'm a little surprised there isn't a single Christmas ornament on the tree or figurines lining the mantle."

Finn points to a stack of boxes in the corner. "We were planning on decorating tonight. It's been a tough season for the boys since their mom passed away, but they're ready to get into the holiday spirit. As far as my parent's home is concerned, you remember that it was my sister who always made the house festive with her love of all things Christmas. Would you and your girls like to help us? We're a bunch of guys without a creative bone in our bodies."

I smile broadly because Christmas has always been my favorite holiday, and I could rival Finn's older sister, Jenny, in the decorating department. Every winter, when she would come home from college, her first order of business was to turn the Hollister home into a winter wonderland.

"We'd love to! Christmas is my jam!" I point in the direction of Ella, who is thoroughly enraptured in a video game with a boy who looks just like Finn did at that age. "That's Ella. She's my oldest at 14 and wants to major in interior design. She'll jump on the opportunity to help. You've already met Ava, who is my youngest and is willing to do anything that can create a mess. Then there's Mia, who is the ten-year-old on the couch, sulking."

Finn mouths the names over and over to commit them to memory. He's a firm believer in the "rule of ten," which is when you say or read something ten times, you'll remember it forever. He points to the three boys gathered around the television. "The oldest is Micah, and he turned 16 last week. He's following in my footsteps and is a junior firefighter in town. The other two are the twins, Isaac and Jonah. Isaac is the one with short, cropped hair, while Jonah has the curly mop."

"All Biblical names," I say, stating the obvious. "I didn't peg you to go that route. I thought when we, um, I mean, you had kids, you'd name them after famous football players."

Finn chuckles. "I didn't get much of a say. I wasn't the one who birthed them after all."

I wave my hand in the direction of the kids. "Surely your opinion counted for something."

"Nope. I suggested names but was quickly overruled," he jokes. "I offered up Jerry for Jerry Rice and Tom for Tom Brady. There was no way she was going to have her twins be called Tom and Jerry."

I chuckle. "No, I guess not. I can't really blame her for putting the kibosh on something like that." I give him a feeble smile that barely covers the hurt. If Micah is 16, that means that Finn left me for another woman or that he the hangup button over and over again, but still nothing. "Come on!"

"What's the problem?" Finn asks, sneaking up behind me.

I wave the phone above my head and accidentally smack my face with the cord. "Ow!" I rub my forehead to numb the sting, "That was a self-critiquing moment if I ever had one," I mumble, my cheeks heating from embarrassment. I hand him the receiver and grumble, "There's no dial tone, Finn. I need to let my parents know we didn't drive off a cliff or get eaten by a bear."

Finn takes the receiver and puts it up to his ear before placing it in the cradle. "Bears are in hibernation, Bailey, so there's no chance of that. Plus, you don't have enough meat on your bones to be a worthy meal or even a light snack."

"Finn, this isn't funny! You know my mom. She'll start coming up with the worst-case scenarios in her head that puts a Bailey-eating bear to shame. Mom will think aliens have abducted us or that I got lost and ended up in Florida."

Finn holds a finger to my mouth. "Shh. Bailey, you need to calm down. I've got you covered." He grabs his walkie-talkie and calls the Chief.

"Chief, this is Hollister," Finn says.

"Hollister, this is Chief. I have you loud and clear. What's your status?"

"The boys and I were able to get to the family in time. They're here at the cabin and riding out the storm with us, but the landline is out. Can you pass on a message to their family and appraise them of the situation?" Finn asks.

"Sure. Who am I contacting?" the fire chief asks.

"Please let Barb and Henry McNamara know that their daughter, *Bailey*, and their grandchildren are safe."

"Hollister, did you just say that Bailey is with you? As in *the* Bailey?"

Finn walks into the other room and closes a set of French doors behind him, but I can still make out his words. "Affirmative. As soon as the storm passes and it's safe to come down the mountain, I'll bring them to town."

"Hollister. Are you sure this is a wise decision considering your history?"

"I don't have a choice, Chief. It's not safe to travel, and they have nowhere else to go. You always go on and on, preaching about learning from our mistakes. I've taken that to heart and don't intend to make the same one twice," Finn says.

I don't wait around to listen to the rest of their conversation, having heard more than enough. Needing to keep myself busy so that I don't dwell on being called a "mistake," I walk over to the kids and tap on Micah's head. He pauses the game and looks up at me. I smile and ask, "Is it okay with you guys if I bust open a box of decorations? I want to make myself useful."

Ella giggles. "Mom can't help herself at Christmas, so be warned! By the time she's done, there won't be an inch of space that doesn't have a figurine, ornament, or wreath."

Mia chimes in from behind the pages of the book she's holding. "Mom also makes the best cookies. I can't wait for this place to smell like a bakery instead of dirty socks."

"Mia! That was rude!" I scold. "We're guests in this home, and you need to apologize."

She places the book on her chest and smiles sweetly at the boys. "I apologize for saying this house smells like dirty socks, even if it's true. Forgive me?"

Isaac and Jonah scowl at my daughter, but Micah laughs. "You're forgiven. If you think it smells like feet now, wait until after we have refried beans at dinner. We're having tacos."

Mia finally smiles slyly at her older sister. "I'm used to Ella passin' gas. She does it so often that Mom has nicknamed her 'Tooter.'"

"Why you!" Ella screams, getting up to tackle Mia for sharing that secret, especially in front of an older boy who is cute to boot. Mia tosses the book and takes off running. Then Ava chases after Ella, thinking they're playing a game of tag. Total chaos ensues as Isaac and Jonah join in, and pillows start flying along with insults and name-calling.

Micah gets up and stands beside me, watching as pure pandemonium unfolds. When he notices me rubbing my temples, he grins and says, "And to think, you can't even spank them without going to jail."

# Chapter Four

## Finn

Chief Zimmerman was a Lieutenant in the fire department when I was a junior firefighter and has been a friend and mentor to me for two decades. He was there for me when my best friend, Daniel, dropped the bomb that he and Bailey were dating and had been getting together behind my back for the entirety of my senior year.

I turn the volume down on the radio and step into the other room. "I don't have a choice, Chief. It's not safe to travel, and they have nowhere else to go. You always go on and on, preaching about learning from our mistakes. I've taken that to heart and don't intend to make the same one twice."

"Is Bailey home for the holidays or for good? I heard through the grapevine that she and Daniel got a divorce. I never liked him much," he says with mild disdain.

I purse my lips in frustration. "How did you hear about that? I figured if the gossip were going to get around town, it would have made its way to me first." There are pros and cons to living in a small town. The pro is that everyone knows your name and will support you in every way. The con is that everyone knows your name, and they aren't afraid to get all up in your business.

I can hear the smile in Zimmerman's voice when he says, "Barb told Joan, who told Alice, who then told Nancy. Nancy told her husband, Bart, who then told me. It's bad enough getting information third-hand. When you're the seventh in line to hear the news, it's bound to be skewed."

I pinch the bridge of my nose while simultaneously hitting the talk key. "It's messed up, that's for sure. However, I can validate that the information is, in fact, correct. Bailey and Daniel got a divorce, and she was driving a food truck, not a car or rental. I'm going out on a limb and saying that she's either home for good or at least planning on staying in one of the local towns. Maybe Ticonderoga?"

"So, Bailey is single, and you're single, trapped in a cabin together for the next few days. Be careful, Buddy. Don't let her beautiful blue eyes ensnare you again," he warns and then amends, "Unless you want to get ensared. Then go for it and know that I'm rooting for you."

I'm not about to tell him it's her lips that have always enticed me. "You don't have to worry about us. There are six kids in the house, which guarantees that there wouldn't be any privacy."

Zimmerman grunts a reply. "Yeah, right. If people can find a way to make out on an airplane with 300 other people, you guys can find a way to be alone."

I growl low and dangerous. "You know me better than that. I'm not that type of guy."

"I know you aren't, and I wasn't trying to imply that you are, Finn. All I meant was that the two of you can find some time alone to work some stuff out. If you're going to be living in the same town, it's better to get some things straightened out. I recommend doing it sooner rather than later."

"You guys realize you're speaking on an open channel, right?" Bryce asks. He's a royal pain in my rear end and is still good friends with Daniel. "You should stay as far away from Bailey as possible, Finn. She's bad news and will only hurt you in the end. She did it before. She'll do it again."

"Thanks for the advice. Hollister out."

# CABIN FEVER WITH MY FIRST FLAME 33

"Hollister!" Bryce yells over the radio. He has more to say, but I'm in no mood to listen.

I ignore Bryce. "Zimmerman, I'm changing frequencies. You know which channel to reach me on if there's another emergency. I'm supposed to be on leave and spending time with the boys."

"Copy, Hollister. Zimmerman out."

I change the channel to a preset frequency that we should have been using in the first place. I have been so focused on the conversation with the chief that I managed to tune out the screaming filtering in from the living room. When I enter, my mouth drops open, and my eyes bulge when Mia swan dives over the back of the couch and lands on top of Isaac, rubbing her sock in his face.

"Mia, that's enough! Get off him right now!" Bailey shouts.

Micah and Ella are bent over laughing, doing nothing to help Bailey gain control of the situation. I don't know what to do, so I stand back and watch. I'll run into a burning building without fear, but pit me against six kids, and I'm out of my depth.

"Isaac started it when he sat on Ava and tooted! He's lucky I didn't have ice cream, or otherwise, it wouldn't be a sock in his face!" Mia shouts, still rubbing her dirty footwear up Isaac's nostrils.

Bailey marches over to the sofa and plucks the sock from Mia's grasp, picking up Mia in the process and separating the two delinquents. Isaac points at Ava, who is red-faced and has tears streaming down her face. "She...She..." he stutters as he prepares to lay blame, realizing that his joke wasn't as funny as he intended.

Isaac walks over to Ava and gives her a hug. Without being told, he apologizes. "I'm sorry."

Ava sniffles and hiccups. "It's all...*hiccup*...all right." Then, she surprises me by returning Isaac's embrace. When she turns away from him, she lifts her leg and lets one rip. The rest of the room absolutely loses it while Bailey shakes her head in dismay.

Bailey starts collecting the couch cushions strewn about the living room, placing them back in their proper spot. When she notices my arrival, her shoulders sag, and she plops down on the sofa. "Finn, I promise you that I have taught my girls to behave better than that. We'll be out of your hair as soon as the storm passes."

I sit on the plush recliner. "It's not a problem, Bailey. The new arrangements will just take a little getting used to. On the plus side, the kids don't seem to have a problem communicating, and your daughters can certainly hold their own."

Bailey cringes. "I've always taught them to stand up for themselves and for others, but I never taught them to use chemical warfare as a form of self-defense." She waves her hand in front of her face. "That's all Daniel."

The kids have calmed down and have glued themselves in front of the video game console; this time, it's Mia and Ava against Isaac and Jonah. Micah begins hauling the boxes of Christmas decorations out while Ella takes the seat next to her mom. "Don't let her fool you, Finn. My mom taught us everything we know."

Bailey blushes but doesn't refute Ella's statement. I've known Bailey for a long time, and although she can be dainty and sweet, she also grew up with her two older brothers, Baxter and Bennett, who now live in Texas. She knows how to fight dirty.

"I'm going to get started on dinner," I say. "I had planned to make tacos. Does that work for you?"

Bailey nods, and Ella grins while elbowing her mother. "Mom loves tacos. She makes the best homemade tortillas, and her salsa is out of this world!"

I hook a thumb over my shoulder in the direction of the kitchen. "The tortillas are in a bag, and the hard shells are in a box. The salsa is from a jar, the cheese is from a resealable container, and the bag of lettuce is pre-shredded. The meat is ground beef that I have to cook, but I use a packet of seasonings that are pre-mixed and cost $1.19 from the store."

Bailey stands up and straightens the sofa cushions. "I can help in the kitchen if you need me to."

Before I can answer, Micah drops the set of lights he's untangling, and his eyes become haunted as they meet Bailey's. "Aren't we going to start decorating?"

Bailey immediately realizes her mistake and doesn't hesitate. "Absolutely, Micah. I'd love nothing more. Why don't we get started?"

Micah smiles and hands Bailey and Ella each a set of lights. They spend the next hour working together to untangle and hang them while I get dinner prepared. The other children have set out figurines, wreaths, and garlands all over the living room and foyer. My inner clean freak is having a meltdown at the mess, especially since it looks like a bomb detonated in the middle of the room. It's only the smiles and laughter from the kids that keep the "tidy monster" from emerging.

"Dinner's ready!" I shout over the loud Christmas music Bailey has blaring through the speakers. We're fortunate that there's anything to eat at all after I almost burned the beef after getting lost in the way Bailey's hips swayed to the music. It was only Micah's goofy grin when he caught me staring that stopped me from ogling Bailey any further. Thankfully, he's the only one who noticed, but I'm sure I'll hear about it later.

Ava jumps up and down, bursting with excitement. "Yay for tacos!" she yells as she barrels into my legs and latches on like a leech. "Thank you, Finn! I'm so hungry I could eat a horse!"

I pick her up and point to the fixings. "Well, all I have is cow. Do you want a hard shell or a soft one?"

Ava pinches her chin, and her tongue pokes out of the side of her mouth as she thinks long and hard about the life-altering decision. "Can I have one of each?"

I grab a paper plate and make her two tacos, but I'm not entirely sure that both will fit in her tiny tummy. After all six kids load up their plates, it's Bailey's turn. She makes only two tacos for herself, but I know that she can put away three if not four. At least, she used to.

"There's plenty to go around. I'm used to preparing meals for an army," I tease. "I usually have to feed ten or more guys at one time when it's my turn to cook at the station."

Bailey smiles hesitantly at me. "Ava might manage to eat one taco before she's full. If she finishes both, I'll be amazed. It's not out of the realm of possibility considering how much she's been running around, but I'm saving room to eat her leftovers so that nothing goes to waste."

"It's just a taco, Bailey. If it ends up in the trash, it's no big deal. Fix what you want," I tell her.

She shakes her head and whispers, "Daniel wouldn't let the family leave the table until every morsel was cleared. If it was served, it was eaten—end of story. We could always go back for seconds if we wanted, but if we put it on our plate, we had to eat it. He always spouted the phrase, 'If you dish it, you eat it.'"

I growl in frustration and step into Bailey's personal space, just shy of our bodies touching. I whisper back, "Bailey, you're not with Daniel anymore. It's time for you to start living again and doing what's best for you and the girls."

She takes a step around me and heads toward the dining room. Just before she turns the corner, she stops and faces me. "I promise I'm trying my best to pick up the pieces of my life and move on, Finn, but it's really none of your concern. I'm a big girl, and like you, I've learned from my mistakes. I, too, never plan on making the same one twice."

# Chapter Five

## Bailey

I'm startled awake by a kick in the head, and I mean that in the literal sense. Ava has somehow managed to do a one-eighty in the bed we're sharing, and her little feet have ended up in my face. Once her little toes start tickling my neck, all bets are off, and any chance of getting back to sleep has gone out the window.

I roll out of bed and stare down at my sleeping angel. "At least one of us got some sleep."

I shuffle downstairs into the kitchen to get a pot of coffee brewing. The house is dark except for a light over the oven, and not a creature is stirring—not even a mouse. I take a moment to enjoy the peace and listen as the wind whips in a frenzy outside.

As I rummage around in the kitchen, I end up making more noise trying to be quiet than I would if I had been banging around. I find the coffee, filters, and purified water with ease, but the contraption in front of me is besting me in every way. I end up talking to myself as I mash 27 buttons, attempting to turn on the coffee pot. "What happened to a good, old-fashioned Mr. Coffee? You just pop in a filter and a few scoops of coffee, then press one button! Voila! Coffee!"

"It helps if you plug it in," says a voice that cracks at the end.

I spin around and clutch my heart, wondering why anyone else would be up at this hour. The clock on the stove taunts me with a big 5:03 in neon green lighting. "Micah, you scared the dookie out of me!"

The teenager, wearing sleep shorts and a band tee, throws his hands up in surrender. "I'm sorry, Mrs. Johnson. I didn't mean to startle you." He points toward the sofa, "I was just sleeping over there and couldn't help but overhear you trying to beat the coffee pot into submission. I thought I could help."

I chuckle. "It's McNamara again, but you can call me Bailey. I apologize if I woke you. It should have been me sleeping on the couch in the first place."

Micah smiles. "It's not a big deal. The sofa is super comfortable." He plugs in the brewer and shows me which buttons to press. I guess when it has power, it's actually user-friendly. Who knew?

Instead of going back to sleep, Micah sits on a stool on the other side of the kitchen island. The kitchen is part of a spacious open floor plan that connects with the living room, kitchen, and informal dining area. There's a formal room area around the corner and to our right, behind a set of French doors, but I prefer the open space. "Micah, aren't you going back to sleep?"

He shrugs. "There's really no point. Finn will be up in less than an hour to do his morning workout in the basement. The clanging of weights is what I use for an alarm clock, and he'll expect me to join him." Micah lowers his gaze. "Is it okay if I have coffee with you?"

I pull out two mugs from the cabinet above the coffee pot. I set one down in front of him while we wait for the brew cycle to finish. "I'd love some company. Hey, do you mind if I ask you a question? You don't have to answer if it makes you feel uneasy."

"I'm an open book. Ask away," he replies.

I lean on the counter, keeping plenty of distance between us so that he doesn't feel like a cornered animal. "How come you call Finn by his name and not Dad?"

"Because that would be weird. Finn didn't ask to be in this position, but he stepped up when our mom got sick. He took us in, packed up our stuff, and moved us here, but he's still adapting to the role of a father figure. Our relationship just isn't like that, no matter how much we love him or he loves us. I doubt we'll ever call him 'Dad.'"

I always pegged Finn to be the doting father, not a man who walked away from his responsibilities. Then again, he walked away from me and that might just be his *modus operandi*. I clearly didn't know him as well as I thought I did.

I smile sadly and reach across the island to squeeze Micah's hand before turning around to grab the coffee pot, not willing to continue talking about a sore subject. However, I feel a burning need to give my condolences. As I pour us each a cup, I tell him, "I'm sorry for your loss, Micah. I know that probably doesn't mean much coming from a total stranger, but it doesn't make it any less true."

"It's okay," he says. "The hardest part about losing my mom is the holidays. She loved Christmas with a passion, and this is the first time she's not with us. Finn is trying to be strong for us, but he's feeling the loss as much as we are. I think he regrets not spending more time with Mom, especially in the final days."

I want to ask what happened, but it seems callous to butt into Micah's personal life when he barely knows me. I take a sip and peer at Micah over the top of the mug. "If there is anything I can do to help while we're here, let me know. If you need a hug, my arms are open. If you need an ear, I'm available to listen."

Micah grins, and there's an impish glint in his eyes that flashes for a nanosecond. "Thanks, Bailey. I'm not much of a hugger, but Finn is. Maybe when you see him, you can wrap your arms around his waist and give him a good squeeze."

I arch an eyebrow in his direction. "I'll take that under advisement. However, I was referring to what I can do to help you, Isaac, and Jonah. Is there anything that I can do to make the holiday a little brighter?"

He thinks about it for a minute and then nods solemnly. "Mia mentioned you bake cookies, and we used to make gingerbread men with my mom every year. Would it be okay if we spent the day doing that?"

"That sounds like a fantastic idea," I tell him. It's a tradition that I have with my girls as well, but six kids in the kitchen is going to be a disaster. Yet, it's a disaster of the best kind. I'll have to warn Finn, who has always kept everything in its place, so much so that he cleaned up last night after the kids went to bed. He started to rearrange the decorations, but that's when I stepped in and stopped him. Cleaning up is one thing. Rearranging the children's hard work and love is another.

"What's a fantastic idea?" Finn asks, interrupting the conversation.

"Bailey is going to make cookies today, and we're going to help," Micah answers for me. It's a good thing, too, because I don't know if I can formulate words with my mouth hanging open and practically salivating at the Adonis in front of me. Finn is shirtless, wearing nothing but a pair of charcoal-gray sweatpants hung low on his hips. The tapered waist and "V" that women obsess over are prominently displayed and getting closer to me with every step. I start to reach out and touch his stomach to verify it's not a figment of my imagination, but I snatch my hand back at the last second.

"How many cookies are we talking about? One sheet?" Finn asks, already calculating in his brain how much of a mess this is going to make.

I laugh, Finn's comment snapping me from the "six-pack-abs haze" I was in. "Surely, you jest. A sheet holds roughly a dozen cookies, Finn. There are six kids and two adults, and five days until Christmas. Even at just one cookie per person per day, that's a three-dozen minimum. No one can eat just *one* cookie. Then there are the quality control samples, the cookies we'll bring into town when you take us to my parents, the ones that end up broken, and…"

"I get it, Bailey. It's going to be a lot of cookies. How many are we talking about?" Finn asks.

I put my hands on my hips and ignore the broad chest in my face as I stare up at Finn. "As many as the kids want, Finn. This is for them. I can promise you that this is going to get messy, and I can guarantee that the younger ones will be wearing more icing than the cookies. But rest assured, I keep a clean kitchen. If I didn't, my restaurant would have failed every health inspection we had. By the time we're finished, your kitchen will be spotless."

"I'll help Bailey clean up," Micah adds before laying on the guilt. "Mom would have wanted us to continue the tradition."

Finn's shoulders slump in resignation, knowing he's been defeated before he can even mount an offense. "Micah, are you going downstairs to work out with me? If so, now would be a great time to get ready. Just be quiet so that you don't wake up Ava when opening your drawers."

"I can work out in what I'm wearing?" Micah says, not getting the hint.

I walk around and rest my hand gently on Micah's arm. "Finn would like to talk to me privately. This is his nice way of asking you to give us a moment."

"Oh. Um. Yeah. I'll just go and get changed. My bad," he retorts apologetically. Before Micah leaves, he leans over and whispers, "This might be the time to give Finn that hug we talked about. He looks like he could use one."

I push him away and laugh. "Get out of here!"

Finn waits until we're alone before he clears his throat. "I haven't seen Micah smile like that since his mom died. Is baking cookies really that important to him?"

I nod and walk around the counter so that I'm face-to-face with Finn and his pectorals once again. "It isn't the cookies themselves that make the kids happy. None of the children need any more sugar, that's for sure. It's the sense of normalcy they get by doing something that once brought them joy, Finn. The girls and I spend all day making cookies to share with the neighborhood and friends. It's what we do. The boys did the same with their mother."

"This could backfire, Bailey. They may end up missing their mom more than ever," Finn argues.

I lift my shoulder in response. "It could, but would that really be so bad? At least, it would be fond memories they're remembering. Or are you the one who would have trouble handling the memories? I'm sure that you loved her immensely."

Finn inhales deeply and squares his shoulders. "Of course I did. She was always there for me and was my best friend. I just wish I had been around more for her."

I had once thought Finn had felt that way about me. Hiding the hurt under a false bravado, I turn my back to him and say, "Then you should understand the importance of keeping her memory alive."

"You're not their mother, Bailey. You don't need to do all this," Finn says with a little bit of bite to his tone.

"You're right, Finn. I'm not. But I can be their friend."

# Chapter Six

## Finn

Bailey offers to make breakfast while Micah and I go through an intense workout in the basement. Between lacrosse and being a junior firefighter, Micah is all about fitness and keeping his body in shape.

We're halfway into our second set of bicep curls when Micah blurts out, "So, what's the deal with you and Bailey? I can't tell whether you want to throw her out into the blizzard or kiss her until you both pass out from lack of oxygen."

"I'm sorry, what? I have no idea what you're talking about."

Micah grins like the Cheshire cat. "Yeah, sure you don't! There is clearly a history between the two of you. I see the way you look at her when you think no one is looking. It's a lot like this." Micah looks off in the distance wistfully and sighs deeply.

I throw my towel at his head. "I do not stare at Bailey like that. We barely know each other." Then, under my breath, I add, "anymore."

Micah starts his last set of reps, huffing and puffing with every curl. "That's not...what...Ella...said. She said...that you...were...high school...sweethearts."

Micah blows out a breath as he replaces the dumbbells on the rack. "Is what Ella told me true?"

I use the bench to do my first set of dips, working the triceps and my core. "You shouldn't believe everything you hear, Micah, and you shouldn't be gossiping."

He comes over and joins me, but instead of doing dips, Micah sits on the floor and stretches out his legs. "You didn't answer me, which is telling in and of itself. Is. It. True?"

"Why does it matter?" I ask.

"Why won't you answer?" Micah snaps back. "Was she the one who got away? Was Bailey the woman that mom always referred to as 'She who shall not be named?'"

I guess our workout is over, and it's time for "guy talk." I grab two bottles of water from the mini fridge and toss one to Micah before sitting down on the floor next to him. "Bailey *is* the one who got away, but that's because I let her go. She broke my heart and is the reason I didn't return to Lake George."

Micah furrows his eyebrows and stares at a small tear in the gym mat. "But Bailey is so tiny and cute. She seems so nice. What happened?"

"It's really not important, Micah. It happened a long time ago, and we've both moved on."

Micah laughs at that. "Have you? You're a perpetual bachelor, Finn. Sure, you've gone on a few dates, but you don't let anyone get close. It's like you held those women to a standard you've set, knowing they'll never measure up."

"I don't have any standards," I retort.

Micah reaches for his toes, bringing his nose to his knees. In a muffled voice, he says, "That's what every teenage boy wants to hear from their male role model."

"That's not what I meant, and you know it. I don't hold women to any set standard, Micah. I let them be who they are. They just weren't meant for me. It's not some secret conspiracy I've concocted to stay single."

"I need some cardio to burn off this energy from being cooped up in the house, not more weightlifting." Micah walks over and hops on the elliptical, leaving me a choice between the treadmill and the stationary bike.

No sooner than I get on the bike and start pedaling, the teenager-turned-therapist picks up right where he left off. "You have to ask yourself why those women were never meant for you."

"Okay, Dr. Ruth. That's enough. Bailey and I didn't work out. It's not that complicated. Let's leave it at that, okay?"

Micah bellows out a laugh. "First off, I have no idea who Dr. Ruth is. Secondly, I'm not leaving it at that. Those women you dated never worked out because you measured them against the 'Bailey Bar'—a bar that was much too high for them to reach. Bailey is upstairs right now, and if anyone can reach that bar, it's the person who set it in the first place. You have an opportunity for a second chance, Finn. Don't waste it."

I stop pedaling and get off the bike, no longer in the mood to continue exercising. Micah takes the hint and stops as well, waiting for me to say whatever it is I'm going to say. "Look, Micah. The truth is she cheated on me with my best friend."

Micah's eyes widen, and he looks toward the ceiling as if he can see through it. Pointing in the general direction of where the kitchen would be, he asks, "You caught Bailey cheating on you? No way!"

"Not exactly. My best friend, Daniel, came clean three months after I left. He told me everything," I admit.

"And what did Bailey say when you confronted her about it?" Micah asks.

I shrug and look down at my shoes. "She never admitted the truth. I called her a few times over the next few months, but every time we talked, she carried on like nothing was amiss. Eventually, I stopped calling. I did write her a letter and told her I was moving to California, but she never wrote me back."

Micah folds his arms across his chest and taps his foot. "Wait. Let me get this straight. You never confronted Bailey about the supposed cheating? You never got her side of the story, even if it was simply to get some closure? You just packed up and left? Man, I'm 16, and I know better than that."

"Hey! It was my best friend who told me the truth. Why would he lie to me?" I ask, annoyed that Micah is right.

He rolls his eyes. "Geeze, I don't know, Finn. Why would your best friend cheat with your girlfriend in the first place? He sounds like a stellar guy and a trustworthy individual to me. I can totally see why you would take him at his word instead of talking to the person who presumably loved you."

"Your sarcasm is duly noted, Micah. What's done is done, and there's no changing the past. Besides, Bailey married Daniel, so there must have been some truth in it." I start cleaning up the gym, wiping down the equipment, and throwing the towels in the hamper.

Micah shakes his head. "You should really talk to Bailey, Finn, even if it hurts in the long run."

"I know you mean well, Micah, but Bailey made her choice, and it wasn't me. A second chance isn't in the cards for either one of us," I tell him as I begin trudging up the stairs.

Micah grins mischievously as he follows behind and I would bet my paycheck that I hear him mutter, "But I know how to stack the deck."

When I get upstairs, I'm greeted by the scent of fresh blueberry muffins baking in the oven and by the sight of Bailey swaying to music I can't hear. Bailey doesn't notice us and starts rummaging through the refrigerator. The top of her body disappears, but her bum continues bouncing to the beat.

Micah pats me on the shoulder on his way to grab clean clothes and a shower, laughing and emitting more sarcasm from his mouth. "And to think, you want to pass up on the opportunity to see that view every day. It's horrific!"

I scowl and push him along. "Shut it, Micah. Go get dressed and then wake up the boys."

"What about the girls?" he asks.

"That's up to Bailey. She's their mom and knows their schedule."

Bailey is still rummaging around in the fridge when I walk up behind her and tap her on her back.

There's a loud *oomph* as Bailey smacks her head on the middle shelf, followed by a crash as a jar of pickles falls to the floor and shatters around her bare feet. Without a second thought, I scoop Bailey into my arms and set her down on a barstool, well out of the danger zone.

She holds up a stick of butter like a trophy as she rubs her head with her free hand. Bailey yells, "Why are you Hollister men always sneaking up on me!"

I pluck the earbuds from her ears and wave them in her face, the muted sound of Christmas music filtering out. "If you weren't jamming to Nat King Cole, you might have heard us. We weren't exactly being quiet."

She holds out her hand, palm flat, silently asking for the earbuds back. "It wasn't Nat King Cole. It was Lauren Daigle singing 'Light of the World,' thank you very much. I was wearing the headphones so that I wouldn't wake everyone up."

I return the earbuds and drop down to one knee to inspect her feet for any cuts. Bailey mock gasps and clutches her heart, "Oh, Finn. It's too soon!"

"Are you getting married?" Isaac asks, shuffling into the kitchen area quietly and wiping away the sleep from his eyes.

"No!" Bailey and I shout in unison. When Isaac's eyes become as wide as dinner plates from the rebuke, I calm my tone and add, "Sorry, Buddy. We didn't mean to yell. I'm just checking Bailey's feet for any cuts, not proposing. There's a broken jar of pickles by the fridge, and your feet are also bare, so I need you to stay out of the kitchen until I clean up."

Bailey smiles at Isaac. "Can you do me a huge favor, Isaac? Can you be the leader and keep everyone else from entering the kitchen? It will be up to you to keep everyone safe and prevent further injuries."

Isaac puffs out his chest. "You can count on me, Mrs. Bailey!"

I lift Bailey's foot and turn it to inspect it for injury, finding a small cut near her heel. "Don't move. I'm going to grab the first aid kit and clean that up for you."

Bailey pulls her foot from my grasp. "I'm fine, Finn. I'm more than capable of applying a bandage to a boo-boo. I've been taking care of myself for a long time, as well as three girls who rough-house and are prone to injury."

I scowl at the idea of Bailey doing everything on her own, even though Daniel was with her. "You shouldn't have had to, Bailey, and right now you don't. You have a sliver of glass that is going to require tweezers to remove. So, unless you are a contortionist or a Master of Yoga, you're going to need my help to get it out."

"Well, what are you waiting for? Let's see you put those EMT skills to use. I've got buns in the oven..." Bailey starts to say when there's a loud shriek, and Ella makes her presence known.

"Mom, are you pregnant?"

# Chapter Seven

## Bailey

Finn gets up to grab the first aid kit, not willing to touch this situation with a ten-foot pole. I can't say that I blame him. If it weren't for the cut on my foot, I'd be hightailing it out of here as well.

"I'm not pregnant, Ella. The 'buns in the oven' are merely a reference to a tray of muffins that are currently baking to perfection. You have to be having…um…uh…"

"Coital bliss? Diddling? Gazzing? Smooshing? Making bacon?" Ella asks, taking pleasure in my discomfort and razzing me about it.

"Uh. Yes? Where do you come up with this stuff?" I ask, my face contorted in a mix of confusion and mild disdain. "I have never heard half of those euphemisms for such a sacred act."

"YouTube," she says flippantly as she tries to enter the kitchen, only to be blocked by Isaac.

Isaac has his legs spread apart and has his arms stretched out as wide as he can reach. Sounding like a cop, he barks out, "This is a restricted zone, Ma'am. You may only enter if you have the proper gear." He points to the glass behind him and then to her feet. "Gear which you do not have. Shoes first. Coffee later."

Ella rubs his head playfully, causing Isaac to scowl. "Alright, Napoleon. I'll go put some shoes on, but don't let all that power go to your head. It's big enough as it is."

"At least my head isn't as big as your mouth!" Isaac shouts back.

"Both of you, cut it out," I tell them using the "Mom" voice. It's the tone that every mother inherently learns and one that brooks no argument. "It's too early for bickering, and I've only had one cup of coffee. If you guys can hold off until I finish my second cup, that would be appreciated."

Ella opens her mouth to retort, but then she just lets it hang there. I turn around to see what catches her attention, only to find that Finn still hasn't bothered to put on a shirt and is carrying a small first aid kit. Ella must have been too surprised by the idea of me being pregnant to have noticed Finn's broad chest and muscular back as he practically ran out of the room. She certainly notices now.

Finn doesn't bother looking up. Once again, he kneels at my feet and becomes wholly focused on cleaning and dressing the wound. I can't help but giggle when the tip of his thumb strokes the bottom of my foot. He glances up, "You're still ticklish, I see."

"Mmhmm." It's been so long since I've felt Finn's touch, and it brings back a flood of memories—memories I had long since repressed. Finn and I sunbathing in our swimsuits by the lake. Finn and I holding hands in the back of his pickup truck while we watch a meteor shower. The two of us stealing kisses under the bleachers after one of his lacrosse games.

My trip down memory lane is interrupted when Mia comes in, holding Ava's hand. "First, this place smelled like dirty socks. Now it smells like pickles. What's next? A backed-up toilet?"

"You smell like a toilet," Jonah says, entering the room behind them. His mop of curls is knotted and standing at full attention.

Mia spins around faster than I can blink, flinging Ava like a rag doll behind her. "Oh, my gosh! What did you do? Did you put your finger in a light socket or something?"

Jonah's face scrunches up in confusion. "No. That would be stupid." My daughter opens her mouth to retort, but I stop her before she escalates the situation.

"Meee-ahh," I warn, drawing out her name so that she knows she's treading on thin ice. "Stow it."

"But..."

"But nothing, Mia!" I square off with my ten-year-old, ready to do battle and knowing I'll win. "I don't care who started it. I'm finishing it. If we're going to be making cookies later together, I need you all to get along."

I point towards Jonah, who is as much of an instigator as his twin brother and my ten-year-old daughter. "If I think for one second that our baking adventure today is going to end up in a food fight, I'll put a kibosh on the whole thing!" I place my hands on my hips and make eye contact with every person in the room. "Is that understood?"

Four sets of puppy dog eyes stare back at me, but only because Ella is smirking and Micah is upstairs taking a shower. Ella walks over and leans in, "That was a great speech, Mom. However, it would have been ten times more effective if you weren't getting doctored up while wearing pajama bottoms covered in cartoon reindeer."

Finn starts laughing but is kind enough not to do it out loud. "I think her pajamas are cute. Ella, can you grab your mother's shoes? I'm almost done," he asks, smiling. Ella does as requested and grabs my pair of winter boots by the front door since my pair of slip-on sneakers are in my backpack upstairs in the bedroom.

Once Finn finishes wrapping my foot, he loosens the laces so that I can slip into my snow boots. He immediately goes to work on his next task of cleaning up the kitchen and the shards of broken glass, declining my offer to help. While the kids use the opportunity to get in some gaming, I use it to admire the way his back muscles flex as he sweeps up the glass and mops the floor.

I don't know how long I end up staring at Finn, but I'm snapped from my overt perusal when the smell of smoke reaches my nostrils, and Isaac screams, "Fire!"

I jump into action and grab the oven mitts on the counter, shutting off the oven and opening the door. Smoke billows out, which sets the smoke alarm off and causes me to cough uncontrollably. Barely able to stay upright, I grab the muffin pan and toss it into the sink before slipping on the freshly-mopped floor.

I windmill my arms to stay upright as my boots have difficulty finding purchase on the slick tile. I accidentally smack Finn in the face as he wraps his arms around my waist reflexively, not only to stop me from flailing, but also to halt my downward trajectory. But instead of just me going down for the count, it's the both of us—Finn twisting his body to cushion my fall.

Finn groans and closes his eyes in pain as I squirm to get off him, my elbow pressing into his gut. When he opens them, our eyes lock, and I can no longer move. I'm caught in the smolder of his dark brown eyes, remembering the countless times he held me in his arms as we sat by a campfire and how it felt to be wrapped up in his warm embrace.

"When I suggested that Finn might need a hug, this isn't exactly what I meant by that statement," Micah says as he peers over the counter while grinning and holding back a laugh.

"Ha! Very funny," I reply, rolling off Finn and getting my feet under me. I turn around to help Finn up, but he's already standing and rubbing his lower back.

"I'm going to grab a hot shower and change so I don't smell like a pickle factory," Finn says. "I'll make breakfast for everyone when I'm done."

Placing my hands on my hips, I frown. "I was planning on cooking as a thank you for rescuing us."

Finn glances at the charred muffins and a warped pan taking up residence in his sink, then back at me. "Are you sure that's a good idea, Bailey? I have a limited supply of pots and pans in the cupboard."

I wave the vestiges of smoke from my face and cough one more time. "I haven't burned anything since high school when I tried to bake you a birthday cake. This was a fluke, Finn, and that's because I was distracted."

Ella snickers. "Yeah, you were distracted by the 'Abs and Pecs' show." It's then that Finn realizes he hasn't put on a shirt, and his upper torso is on full display.

Finn blushes, but his cheeks redden even further when Micah adds, "Wait until he flexes his biceps. Ladies are lining up around the block to buy the Christmas Firefighter Calendars because he's Mr. July, shirtless and holding a cute dalmatian puppy. Calendars came out last month and are $20 a pop to raise money for families who lose everything in a fire."

Finn points toward the living room. "Don't you kids have a game to play or an argument to start?"

Micah and Ella both snicker but don't hesitate to head toward the gaming console. Isaac is still diligently standing guard, so I walk over to him and say, "You did a great job, Kiddo. Your warning saved us all. For all your hard work, you get to choose what's for breakfast."

Isaac puffs out his chest, proud he could be of service. "Can we have snowman pancakes and scrambled eggs?"

"Sure thing. Do you want to help or hang out with everyone else in the living room?" I ask.

Isaac's eyes brighten and dance with delight. "I want to help! I'm really good at cracking eggs."

I pull out the two cartons of eggs from the refrigerator that are thankfully on the top shelf and not the middle one that needs fixing. I search for a large mixing bowl and find one just out of my reach. Finn notices my dilemma and grabs it for me.

"Thank you," I tell him, then shooing him out of the kitchen. It's then that I realize I have a problem and chase after him. "Finn, wait! I don't know how I'm going to make cookies without a few more sticks of butter and extra eggs." I lower my voice so the kids don't overhear, "I'm going to have to renege on a promise, and I've never done that before."

Finn's face twists in a mask of confusion. "Yes, you have, Bailey. You broke your promise to me."

Now, it's my turn to be confused. "No, I didn't. You broke your promise to me! You're the one who left and never came back!"

Finn turns his back. "You didn't give me a reason to, Bailey, but it's all water under the bridge now. If you need extra eggs, butter, milk, and staples, ask Micah to show you where we store them in the fridge downstairs."

He continues walking down the hall, not giving me a chance to respond. I stand there for a long minute with my jaw hanging by my ankles, flabbergasted that Finn is blaming me for our break-up. *What did I do to make him think I broke my promise to him?*

I don't have the answer to that, but you can bet your bottom dollar that I'm going to find out.

## Chapter Eight

### Finn

I TAKE LONGER IN the shower than necessary, but I figure it's safe enough to do so since I'm not hearing a smoke alarm blare or the kids shouting at one another. In fact, I hear the faint sound of laughter coming from the living room and kitchen area. It's a sound I could get used to despite my long-standing bachelor status and my preference for peace and quiet.

As I towel dry my hair, I think about the full house and the feisty woman in my kitchen. I'll be the first to admit that it's a new experience for me, as is being a father figure. I don't know the first thing about being a parent or taking care of anyone other than myself. Being a firefighter is one thing, but it doesn't require that I put a roof over someone's head or feed them three meals a day. Yet, I find myself wanting to take care of Bailey and the kids—all six of them.

Micah is right about one thing, although I'll never tell him that since it will go straight to his head, and he'll lord it over me. It's true that I've never gone on more than three dates with a woman since Bailey and I parted ways. Bailey was perfect for me in every way, and no one has come close to measuring up. As Micah put it, "The Bailey Bar" had been set, and there was only one person who could reach it.

I throw on a pair of jeans and a black T-shirt before looking out the window to check the weather. I need to get Bailey and her girls down the mountain and out of my house before I do something foolish, like kiss Bailey senseless and lose my heart all over again. I still haven't fully recovered from the first time.

Drawing back the curtain, I frown. It's still snowing, and the wind has caused drifts that are slowly creeping up the side of the house. By my best estimate, there is nearly five feet of fresh powder on the ground, and the chances of getting out of here are nil.

More laughter greets me as I come down the hall and enter the kitchen to a plethora of smiling faces—some of which are covered in flour. Jonah is the first to see me and grins, "Hey, Finn! We're making pancakes from scratch! I'm going to put chocolate chips in mine!"

"That sounds delicious. What should I put in mine?" I ask him.

"Bailey said you used to use your pancakes to make breakfast tacos filled with eggs and bacon," Isaac interjects. "Bailey has a sheet of bacon in the oven, and Ella is scrambling eggs! I'm going to try one of those!"

I go and stand next to Bailey, who is hovering over a large griddle and adding fresh ingredients to each of the pancakes. There are bowls of blueberries, small banana chunks, chopped walnuts, chocolate chips, and diced strawberries. I lean against the counter and fold my arms across my chest. "I can't believe you remember how I eat pancakes."

She doesn't look at me when she replies, "It's hard to forget when we made them every Saturday morning for three years. Although those pancakes were from a box mix and needed all the help they could get to make them palatable. If you prefer something different now, that's okay."

I can't help but wonder if she's talking about more than the pancakes. "Nope. I'm a creature of habit. I tend to stick with something as long as it's good."

Bailey begins flipping the flapjacks, which are light and fluffy with a beautiful golden-brown top. "Sure you do; until something comes along that's even better. Then it's bye-bye pancakes without so much as an explanation."

"Bailey..."

She holds up her hand and shakes her head. "It's fine," she chokes out. "Like you said, 'It's water under the bridge,' and I shouldn't have brought it up. I'm sorry." She turns her back to me and goes into full mom mode while addressing the children. "Thank you all for your help this morning. This is going to be an amazing breakfast because it was made with love and fun sprinkled in. Now, who is ready to wash their hands so that we can eat?"

Jonah, Isaac, Mia, and Ava all raise their hands and bounce on their toes. Micah grins and offers to help the younger kids accomplish their tasks.

Ella hands me the spatula to take over her duty of scrambling eggs, winking as she does it. As she leaves, she whispers, "Use the alone time wisely, Finn."

The kids go to the bathroom to clean up, and once it's just Bailey and me, I clear my throat. "About what I said earlier, I apologize."

"Which time are you apologizing for? Are you talking about in the hallway when you accused me of breaking my promise to you? Which I never did, by the way. Or are you referring to a minute ago when you implied that I wasn't good enough to stick with?"

I push around the eggs, not sure how to answer. When she tries to reach for the platter in the cupboard above the stove, I press my body against hers and grab it for her. I bring my mouth close to her ear and say in a husky tone, "Both."

Her skin erupts in goosebumps, just like it used to when I whispered sweet nothings to her. But instead of turning around and kissing me like she had in the past, she elbows me in the ribs to move me out of her way. As she's plating the pancakes, she waves her spatula in my face. "We were going to get married, Finn! All you had to do was return home as planned and wait for me to graduate. But *noooooo*! You gave me some cockamamie excuse about a job offer in California that you couldn't refuse and left without so much as a word. Sure, you wrote me a letter, but that doesn't count. It was cowardly and beneath you!"

It was cowardly, but that was because I was devastated when Daniel told me what happened between him and Bailey. "Why would I have come back after what you did?"

She grabs the pan of scrambled eggs and dumps them in a bowl. She immediately goes to the sink and starts rinsing it off to put in the dishwasher. "What, pray tell, is it that I did that warranted a 'Dear John' letter and you ghosting me? You were my best friend? We talked about everything,

Finn. What did I do that was so bad that you couldn't come to me so we could work it out?"

As soon as I open my mouth to finally let out what I've been holding in for 18 years, the buzzer on the oven goes off, and Bailey pulls out a pan of perfectly cooked bacon. It's crisp enough that it doesn't fall limp when you hold it, but it also doesn't crumble in your hand. The wonderful smell momentarily distracts me, as does the pitter-pattering of feet running down the hall.

"We're all clean!" Ava yells, trailing behind Mia, Isaac, and Jonah. There are two teenagers who are conspicuously missing, and I go in search of them. It's not as if Bailey and I can continue our conversation in present company. I peek down the hall and notice that Ella and Micah's foreheads are touching as they whisper conspiratorially and laugh.

Oblivious to my approach, Ella gives Micah two thumbs up and turns in my direction. Ella pulls up short when she nearly plows into me. I gesture between her and Micah, who isn't far behind. "What were the two of you talking about? What's so funny?"

Micah slings an arm around Ella's shoulders and grins. "I was just telling Ella about our Christmas wish list tradition that Mom started when I was born."

"Your mom had a great many traditions at Christmas," I say. "It was her favorite time of year. Which one were you specifically discussing?"

Ella smiles, and it doesn't escape my notice that she hasn't moved Micah's arm off her shoulders. I glance back and forth between Micah and his arm, raising an eyebrow in question. Micah shakes his head like I'm being ridiculous but removes the offending appendage while Ella explains, "Micah was telling me about the letter you write to God. The one where you tell Him the one non-tangible thing you want for Christmas and then place the letter on the tree. On Christmas Eve, you open it and read it aloud so that He hears your request. It's a neat way to pray."

"And that's funny, how?" I ask, turning my body so they can pass by me and head to breakfast. I follow them to make sure they get to their destination without any further detours or delays. My stomach is rumbling, and these two are standing between my breakfast taco and me.

At the end of the hallway, Micah looks over his shoulder at me with a smirk and his eyes dancing with mischief. "The funny part is that Ella and I both want the same thing."

"Wi-Fi?" I joke.

Ella spins around and cocks her head to the side. "That reminds me. How is it that you survive up here without the internet or cell service? How do you communicate with the rest of the world?"

I laugh and usher them into the dining room, which is now loaded with enough food to feed the entire population of Lake George. I sit at the head of the table and wait for the kids to fill their plates. "We've been staying at my parents' house since we relocated here right before the start of the school year. It took over two months before I closed the deal on our humble abode, and we moved in a little less than a month ago. Unfortunately, it used to be a rustic getaway where people were expected to disconnect from the outside world. That means that the internet company is going to have to lay down fiber optic wiring, which they can't do until the ground thaws. It also means we won't have Wi-Fi until late March or early April if we're lucky."

"It's why we can only play against each other on the gaming console and not against other people. We're off-line," Micah says. He's always been an upbeat kid, but I can hear the disappointment in his tone that he won't be able to play against his friends back in California unless he's at my parents' house.

Isaac and Jonah both have ear-to-ear smiles. "But now you get to play with us!" Jonah exclaims.

Micah rubs his curly mop and winks. "Yeah, Buddy. I do."

When Bailey finally sits down and fixes herself a plate, I again notice that her portions are small. Her eyes meet mine, and they silently beg me not to say anything. She engages with the kids, talking about what cookies they are going to make after breakfast. Gingerbread and shortbread cookies top the list because of the icing adventure that occurs once the treat has cooled. I've always been partial to chocolate chip no matter what time of year it is, but I keep my opinion to myself since today is about the kids doing something they love.

Micah and Ella are the first to finish, and they wrangle up the rest of the monkeys to help clear the dishes. Bailey grabs Ava's plate and places it in front of her, finishing off the other half of two pancakes stacked on top of one another and a few bites of scrambled eggs. There's one strip of bacon left on the platter that she stares at longingly, but she gestures for me to take it.

"I know you believe that bacon should be its own food group, Finn. Go ahead and take it so that I can clear the rest of the dishes," she tells me. It's the first word she has spoken to me since our conversation earlier was interrupted.

I stand up and stack the few remaining dishes, taking the strip of bacon and placing it on her plate. "You can have the last piece, Bailey. I'll take care of the clean-up since I have six dishwashers available to help. Sit, relax, and breathe."

She sighs and gives me a timid smile. "Sometimes I think I've forgotten how to do that. Thank you, Finn."

I take a load of dishes into the kitchen and notice all the kids huddled together by the Christmas tree and not by the gaming console like I expected. When they notice me watching them like a hawk, they all giggle before scattering like a bunch of mice.

Ella and Micah come over and give me a hand—Micah bumping me out of the way to get to the sink. After turning the water on, he asks, "Why don't you and Bailey spend some time getting reacquainted? Ella and I will do the dishes. Mia is going to read to Ava while Isaac and Jonah are going to dig through Mom's box of kitchen supplies you have stored in the basement."

I spread my feet and cross my arms, glaring at the pair of teens. "What are you guys up to? Micah, you've never once volunteered to do dishes."

He shrugs. "Last I checked, I was up to 5'11" and still growing. Look, Finn. We just want to do something nice for you. Bailey is going to help us bake cookies, and you can help clean up that mess. Let's just call it even."

Not wanting to look a gift horse in the mouth, I do an about-face and head back toward the dining room. When I pass through the open French doors, I halt in my tracks when I notice that Bailey is crying.

She doesn't look at me although she heard me enter the room. "Finn, I know how much you hate to see a girl cry, so I'm going to spare you the awkwardness. I'm fine, but I just need a few minutes alone."

## Chapter Nine

### Bailey

FINN STANDS AT THE entrance to the dining room even though I told him I need a moment alone. If I turn around and meet his gaze, I'm sure he'll look like a deer caught in headlights. Finn has never been comfortable with a woman crying, which is why he always went out of his way to ensure that I never did.

"Really, Finn, I'll be okay," I tell him, hoping he'll go back the way he came. "You told me to sit back, relax, and breathe. This is why I don't. If I stop for even a moment, the world feels like it's crashing in on me."

Instead of hearing the soft shuffle of Finn's feet moving away, they come closer. Eventually, he occupies the seat closest to me. I bury my face in my hands and burst into more tears. He gently pulls my arms so that I'm forced to look at him with my puffy red eyes and runny nose. "Bailey, talk to me. What's going on?"

"Life, Finn. That's all. I'm fine," I tell him.

Finn chuckles, but not at my expense. "Is 'fine' a code word for a woman who broke down on the side of the road in the middle of a snowstorm, only to be rescued by the one person she never thought she would see again? In this case, I'm sure that 'fine' means 'I'm about to have a full-on meltdown.'"

"I wish I could say that you're wrong, but that's pretty spot on. I've had to be strong for the girls, but I haven't really had a moment alone to process the divorce, the move, or starting all over. I feel like such a failure."

Finn takes my hand in his and gently rubs tiny circles near the base of my thumb. It used to calm me down, but now it's just making my heart beat twice as fast. "Can I ask why you and Daniel got a divorce?"

"Do I have to answer?"

Finn shakes his head. "No. I'd never force you to do anything you don't want to, Bailey. I just feel like you might need someone to talk to. We might not be friends exactly, but we aren't enemies, are we?"

I don't answer his question, but I do start spilling my guts. "It's not all that complicated. Daniel fell out of love with me. Even though we worked together eight hours out of the day running a restaurant, I was the one who took the girls to their sporting events, cheerleading practice, and dance recitals. By the time Daniel got home from work—because he often stayed late to do the books and place the orders—we were both emotionally spent and physically drained. It didn't leave a whole lot of room for romance, if you know what I mean."

Finn gently squeezes my hand, and I pull it back. His touch, as much as I want it or need it right now, isn't going to help my state of mind. His face falls, but then he schools his features and leans back in his seat to put a little distance between us. "I know you wouldn't give up so easily, Bailey. You've always been a fighter."

"I didn't. Even after I found out the real reason he was staying late at work, I begged and pleaded to go to counseling or for us to take a vacation with just the two of us and leave the kids with Pops and Nana. Instead of giving me either one of those things, he served me with divorce papers, sold the restaurant, and got engaged to the hostess."

Finn's body tenses, and anger courses through his veins. "What? How could he have done that without your signature?"

"He forged it. It would have cost me more in legal fees to take him to court, but in the end, I won that battle without having to lift a finger. Daniel used the money to pay off the mortgage on the house because he planned on keeping it in the divorce. He offered to let me keep the food truck, but it wasn't ours because my parents paid for it as an investment in the restaurant and in me. Technically, it's theirs. In the end, the house is being sold, and we have to pay off the credit cards first. After that, we'll split the profit down the middle, and the girls and I will get our fresh start."

"A start that is delayed by a snowstorm that isn't letting up. From the looks of things, it might be another day or two before it's safe to take you into town," Finn tells me. "If the second storm hits and is as bad as this one, we might have to dig our way out of here. There's already five feet of snow on the ground and more coming."

I pinch the bridge of my nose and inhale deeply. "I'm sorry that you got stuck with us. I doubt this was how you planned to spend the holidays."

Finn smiles at that. "It's been an adventure so far, and the kids seem to be getting along for the most part."

"We are, too, for the most part. I'm glad we can keep it cordial."

Finn's lips turn upside down, and he's silent for a minute before he finally speaks. "I'm actually a little surprised by that. I knew that when I packed up the boys and moved them here, there would be a good chance that our paths would cross eventually. Lake George is too small for that not to happen, even if you only came home for a visit. I thought for sure that we would either have a blow-out argument or do everything in our power to steer clear of one another."

"It's been 18 years since you left. That's more than enough time for us to let go of any grudges, perceived or otherwise, Finn. I stopped being angry with you a long time ago. Heck, I'm not even angry at Daniel. Hurt, yes. Angry, no."

Rapping his fingers on the table, Finn contemplates my words. "Do you still love him?"

"Daniel? Of course, I do. He's the father of my children and will be a part of their lives as long as they want him to be. But if you're asking whether or not I'm *in* love with him, the answer is 'No.' When someone cheats on you, it has this uncanny ability to taint the relationship. Love isn't turned off with a flip of the switch just because someone hurt you, Finn. However, it changes you from the inside out, and in turn, the love changes accordingly. For some people, it turns to hate. For others, they become indifferent. I don't have the luxury of either because I have three girls who love their father unconditionally, and I need to be their role model. I need to show them that forgiveness is possible no matter how much someone hurts you."

"That's easier said than done, especially when someone cheats on you," Finn says, devoid of emotion.

I reach over and grasp his hand in solidarity, but it's him who pulls away this time. I fiddle with the hem of my shirt, not knowing what to do with my hands. "I'm sorry that you had to experience that kind of heartache. Whoever she is, she's an idiot for doing that to you."

Finn's tone becomes as cold as the weather outside. "Is that your way of apologizing to me for breaking my heart, Bailey?"

"What? Finn, are you implying that I'm the one who cheated on you? Because if that's true, then you are sorely mistaken. I waited for you, faithfully, I might add. Even after the letter you sent as a graduation gift, I still waited another six months, praying for your return. After a year of you being gone, I gave up any shred of hope I had that you still loved me."

Finn's face becomes ashen as my words sink in. "Daniel told me that the two of you had been secretly getting together the entirety of my senior year. He's the one who told me to stay away because it would make things awkward."

"And you believed him?" I screech. "I spent every waking moment with you, Finn! When would I have had time to spend with Daniel while I was dating you? The only time I ever saw him is when the three of us hung out together or when he tutored me in physics."

Finn mumbles, "He was my best friend, and I didn't think he would lie to me." His argument is weak, and he knows it.

My tears try to make another appearance, but I force them back. "I was your best friend, too, Finn. I was supposed to be your life-long partner. You were supposed to trust me and talk to me."

"I tried, Bailey, but I couldn't bring myself to ask you the question. I kept waiting for you to admit the truth and break things off with me, but you didn't. Then everyone I talked to said that you and Daniel were spending a lot of time together, and...well, in my mind, it only confirmed what Daniel had told me."

I stand up and push my chair underneath the table. "It confirmed nothing other than that Daniel and I were friends and that you didn't trust me, Finn. If you couldn't communicate with me then and lacked faith in me, then what kind of marriage would we have had? Maybe it was best that you left when you did, and everything worked out as it should have."

I turn to leave, not sure how to process the revelation that Finn thought I had cheated on him. I've always tried my best to be honest, loyal, and trustworthy so that my word actually means something. I don't get far before Finn catches up and blocks my path.

Finn rubs the side of my arm and lifts my chin so that my gaze meets his. "Bailey, I'm truly sorry. If I could go back and change the past, I would do things differently. I was young, dumb, and foolish, and I let go of the best thing to ever happen to me. I know this isn't going to mean much to you now, but all I ever wanted was for you to be happy, and I never wanted to stand in the way of that. Please forgive me."

The earnest expression on Finn's face tugs at my heart. He made a mistake that cost us both dearly, but I firmly believe that God lets everything happen for a reason—including my heartache. If things hadn't turned out the way they did, I wouldn't have my three amazing daughters, whom I love with every ounce of my being. Finn wouldn't have fallen in love with someone else and had three boys who are a ton of fun.

I stand on my tiptoes and wrap my arms around Finn's neck to pull his ear close to my lips. "I forgave you a long time ago."

# Chapter Ten

## Finn

I STAND IN THE dining room and watch Bailey depart, wondering how I could have been so ignorant all of these years. I should have known that she wouldn't have betrayed me, but then again, I didn't think that Daniel would have either. For years, I've been harboring a grudge because our "friend" had manipulated Bailey and me, but I still have no idea as to why he would have done such a thing.

I don't know how long I spend trying to unravel the mysteries of the universe and coming up short, but eventually, Micah joins me in the dining room. He waves his hand in front of my face, pulling me from wayward thoughts. "What happened between you and Bailey? Please tell me you begged her for a second chance and then kissed her!"

I put up my hands to stop him. "I did neither of those things, Micah. Bailey and I needed to work some things out first."

Micah smirks. "Lemme guess, you confronted Bailey and found out that she never cheated on you and that your once best friend Derrick lied to you so that he could get the girl."

"His name is Daniel."

"Who cares what his name is? He lost the girl, and now you can swoop in and save the day! You are an elite firefighter who parachutes out of airplanes and helicopters. You run into burning buildings to pull people from the fire. Rescuing a damsel in distress is part of your job description." Micah continues to wax poetic about princes saving the princesses from evil beasts and of star-crossed lovers finding each other because it's their destiny.

"Seriously, Dude, what are they making you read at school?" I ask. Until now, I didn't know that Micah had a romantic bone in his body. Then it hits me, and I turn the tables on him. "Do you have a thing for Ella?"

Micah turns several shades of pink in under a second. "No! Ella is pretty, and she's a blast to hang out with, but she's more 'friend' material at this stage in my life. I need someone older, wiser, and more mature."

"Uh-huh."

"Seriously, Finn. I like Avory Mills from my science class. We have chemistry together, if you get my drift." He winks, and it looks like he has something in his eye. I'm going to have to work with him on that, especially if he wants this Avory girl to laugh with him and not at him. "Where were we? Oh, that's right, Finn. We were discussing your lack of a love life, not mine."

I sigh. "Micah, Bailey is here for a fresh start, not a repeat performance of the past. Now that I know the truth and that one simple question would have changed everything, I'd love a second chance with Bailey. I just don't think she's ready to give me one since she's dealing with a lot at the moment. I'd settle for being friends now that we've cleared the air."

"You just leave the romance to us," Micah says. "Go with the flow, and we'll ensure you get your do-over."

"Um. No. Absolutely not!"

Micah rests his elbow on my shoulder, which isn't difficult to do since he's almost as tall as me. "Look, Finn. I know you think we're just a bunch of kids who don't have a clue about romance, but let's face it, neither do you. You're going to need our help whether you want it or not."

I scowl at the over-confident teenager with a penchant for being happy. "I'm perfectly capable of romancing Bailey on my own."

Micah laughs. "You're a stud, no doubt about it. But she doesn't want to be swept off her feet. She wants her feet *rubbed*. She wants to be trusted, supported, and appreciated. That's the type of rescue Bailey needs."

Christmas music starts blaring from the living room, and a chorus of voices singing off-key hits my ears. Instead of cringing from the noise, I find myself smiling, tapping my foot, and bobbing my head. Micah glances at my feet and grins, waiting for me to admit the truth.

"All right, Micah. You win. What do you have in mind?"

"Trust me, you don't want to know," he replies, waggling his eyebrows and rubbing his hands together in excitement. "Seriously, Finn, all you need to do is be yourself. Let us handle the rest."

"It's what 'the rest' entails that has me worried," I mumble. "Micah, don't you have somewhere to be? Aren't you supposed to be making cookies or something?"

He gestures in the direction of the kitchen. "Ella and I agreed that the younger kids would have more fun making the dough. It's not as if we can all fit into the kitchen without it turning into a full-blown circus act. Besides, once Isaac and Jonah were old enough to help Mom, I was promoted to being the 'Quality Control Specialist' and

'Decorating Coordinator.' It's my assigned position in the hierarchy in the kingdom of cookie confections."

I chuckle. "That used to be my role and my favorite part, but that's also because your mom knew if she didn't keep me out of the kitchen while she was baking, the chocolate chips and other ingredients would disappear before they ever got mixed into the dough."

I finish cleaning up the last of the dishes on the table and follow Micah toward the kitchen. I nearly drop the plates in my hand as I double over in laughter at the sight before me. Bailey knows my penchant for tidiness and has taken precautionary measures to mitigate the potential mess.

Isaac, Jonah, Mia, and Ava are all wearing black garbage bags with holes cut out for their heads and arms. The bottom of the bags are folded up and duct-taped on the sides to create makeshift pockets to catch ingredients instead of those ingredients ending up on the floor.

I sidle up next to Bailey, who is currently mixing a batch of gingerbread dough by hand. "I'll admit, Bailey, that was an ingenious idea to use trash bags as aprons. I don't know if I would have thought to do that."

She doesn't look at me, but the corner of her mouth lifts. "You wouldn't have had to. I saw the packages of premade cookies you have in the freezer downstairs. No mess. No fuss. How very *Finn-like*," she teases.

"They taste the same," I say, knowing full well that I'm putting my life in jeopardy with that comment.

The look of horror that crosses Bailey's face is priceless. She stops mixing and turns to face me. "That's blasphemous! You take that back!" she exclaims, waving the mixing spoon around in the air. "Store-bought is *never* better than homemade!"

"If Finn is cooking, it is," Isaac says in all seriousness. "That's why almost everything he makes comes from a can, bag, or box."

Jonah nods solemnly. "If Finn tried to make something from scratch, we'd all starve."

Bailey whips her utensil in my direction and accidentally flings a piece of dough that hits me squarely between the eyes. I'm stunned by the impact, but Bailey doesn't register what happened as she continues her rant. "As long as I'm here, the use of pre-packaged food will be used as a last resort."

Ella cups her hands around her mouth and shouts, "Shots fired! Take cover!"

"What? Why?" Bailey asks, not understanding the nature of Ella's warning. Bailey finally registers what happened when she notices me wiping goop from my face. "Oh, my goodness. I'm so sorry, Finn."

"You will be," I say in a menacing voice, but also with the corners of my mouth turned upward. I stalk toward her, and she takes a few hesitant steps backward. When I close the distance, she whispers, "Don't you dare."

"Oh, I dare," I tease, snatching the cookie dough-coated spoon from her grasp and running it down the side of her face. "Now, we're a matching pair," I whisper back. Our gazes lock, and I use the pad of my thumb to caress her cheek, neither one of us caring that I'm smearing gingerbread all over her face.

Ignoring the world around us, she casts her eyes downward and mumbles, "You're making a mess of things, Finn."

"I'll clean it up, Bailey. If you'll allow it, I'll make things right."

She shakes her head and takes one more step back, causing my hand to fall by my side. Before she can get her next words out, the moment is broken by Jonah shouting, "Food fight!"

We both spin on our heels and raise our hands, shouting in unison, "NO!"

Bailey takes it one step further, "If one crumb leaves your hand, Jonah, you'll be the one who has to clean the kitchen." She makes eye contact with every single person in the room, including me. "That goes for all of you!"

Ella leans down and whispers something in Jonah's ear, causing him to giggle and grin. Jonah walks over to Bailey and wraps his arms around her waist. Looking up at her, he says, "I'm sorry, Bailey. Food isn't meant for fighting. It's meant to show our love. We're going to make a lot of love."

Bailey fights back a laugh and hugs Jonah back. "Yes, we're going to *show* our love through baking. Why don't we get back to it?"

"Is there anything I can do to help?" I ask. I don't want to be useless, but I also don't want to take away any joy from the kids.

Bailey points to the refrigerator. "The middle shelf still needs to be fixed, and if you have a mixer stand handy, that will save us a ton of time."

"The shelf I can do, but you're out of luck with a mixer stand. I've never had a need for one." I open up the refrigerator and begin removing the items so that I can reattach the shelf. I flex my biceps for her and grin. "I can help stir if your arms get tired."

Bailey wraps the bowl with plastic wrap and heads toward the front door. I ask her where she's going, and she points toward the bowl. "There isn't enough room to chill this in the refrigerator, and we have several more batches to make. Setting it outside for an hour or two should work like a charm."

Before I can stop her, Bailey opens the front door and comes face-to-face with a pile of snow up to her chin. Her mouth drops open, and she just stands there in shock from the amount of fresh powder that has fallen in the past 24 hours. If that isn't bad enough, the wind blows Bailey's hair back and gifts her with a face full of frozen flakes.

I run over and shut the door, then take the bowl from the statue standing in front of me. I laugh as Bailey blinks rapidly, processing the magnitude of the storm outside. "You're not supposed to eat the snow," I joke.

Bailey shakes out her hair and wipes her face. "I guess I should be grateful it wasn't yellow."

# Chapter Eleven

## Bailey

Finn gets a roaring fire going in the fireplace, and I take a few minutes to sit near the heat and thaw out before resuming my duties in the kitchen. For the next couple of hours, the eight of us operate like a well-oiled machine. Ella and Micah help the younger kids measure out the dry ingredients while Finn whips the softened butter for me.

By the time we're finished, six bowls of dough need to be refrigerated. Micah suggests putting them on the back porch, which is blocked by the wind and doesn't have over five feet of snow blocking the exit.

"How come we have to wait to cut out the cookies?" Isaac asks. "I don't remember Mom making us wait."

Micah jumps to my rescue and answers for me, "That's because Mom would make a batch the night before so that it was ready right away. It was her little secret."

"That's actually a great idea. I never thought about doing that," I tell them. "If you want to come over to our house next year and help us make cookies, I'll make sure to have some ready."

"That would be awesome!" the twins exclaim in unison.

Finn's radio squawks in the other room, and he excuses himself while I sit with the kids and take a breather. "Is anyone up for playing a game?" I ask.

"When aren't we?" Micah retorts. "We have first-person shooter games, strategy games, and racing games."

Ella giggles. "My mom is referring to board games. She doesn't know the first thing about playing video games or how to use a controller."

"Oh. We have a few in the hall closet," Micah says as he starts to get up.

I wave my hands, indicating he should sit back down. "I can get it."

Micah's brows furrow. "Are you sure? The board games are on the top shelf."

"I'm short, but not *that* short! How about I'll call you if I need any help?" Micah is a sweet kid, and he'll be a good influence on Ella when school starts after the holidays. I'm glad Ella will have a friend and someone to show her the ropes. Mia won't care and prefers to keep to herself, while Ava has never had a problem making friends.

I head down the hallway and open the closet, perusing the games on the top shelf. Pictionary seems to be the best bet since it can be played with teams and is always good for a laugh. I'm once again forced to stand on the tips of my toes in order to reach it. Just when I think I've got it, a giant hand hovers above me and nabs it.

I spin around and come face-to-face with Finn's broad chest, clad in a black, form-fitting T-shirt that hugs all his muscles. They've been difficult to ignore all morning, but I've been sneaking in peeks here and there and admiring the view. There's no ignoring them now, and I involuntarily lick my lips.

Finn's eyes darken when the tip of my tongue slowly glides across my bottom lip, and he takes a small step forward. "Do you like what you see, Bailey?"

"Hmm?"

He chuckles lightly. "I asked if you like what you see."

"It's not bad if you're into muscular physiques and bulky biceps. Which I'm not, by the way. I just don't remember your muscles being quite so big or your chest so broad."

"And what are you into, Bailey Bug?" he asks huskily, using his nickname for me. I told him not to do it, but for some reason, I can't bring myself to chastise him for it at this moment. I've always loved the way the name rolled off his tongue, mainly because he always used it as a sign of affection. And as much as I don't want to admit it, I need affection—even if it's just verbally.

"Short and scrawny. Then I don't have to look up and get a crick in my neck."

"I can massage your neck for you," Finn offers and then runs the tip of his finger from my neck, across my shoulder, and down to my wrist. He entwines his fingers with mine and brings my hand up to his lips. I almost take him up on his offer, but then he smiles, and I can't tell if he's joking or being serious. I'm in the mood for a game, but not the kind he's playing.

"As lovely as that sounds, a hot bath would also do the trick." I take the Pictionary box from his hands and change the subject as fast as I can. "What was the call on the radio all about?"

Finn steps back to give me some breathing room and walks beside me into the living room. "Chief was informing me that the town has seven feet of snow, and the plows are barely keeping up. New York, as well as our tiny town, has entered into a state of emergency and the governor has mandated that everyone is to shelter in place for the time being."

"Were they calling you in?" I ask.

"No, but I'll need to start digging a path to the garage soon in case he does. The snowmobiles and ATVs are parked inside. Chief Zimmerman just called to give me an update and check up on us. By the way, your parents say 'Hi!' and they can't wait to see you and the girls."

"Do you need any help shoveling snow?" Micah asks as we enter into the living room.

Finn nods. "Eventually, but I think we have a game to play first. Who's up for some Pictionary?"

"What's Pictionary?" Isaac asks, looking at the game with apprehension. "It sounds boring."

"It's so much fun!" Mia beams. She explains the rules and we split into two teams, girls against boys. Finn finds a ream of blank computer paper and some markers, and we spend the next two hours laughing our pants off.

"How did you not guess that I was drawing a firefighter, Finn?" Jonah asks, disappointed that the boys lost the game because his team didn't give the correct answer. "I drew YOU!"

I giggle as Finn and Micah both try to worm their way out of this one. Jonah's picture looks nothing like a firefighter. Finn studies the picture carefully and then grins. "I see it now! I was looking at it from the wrong angle."

Isaac laughs uproariously. "Jonah, it's a cowboy stick figure peeing on a bush!"

Jonah frowns. "No, it's not! It's Finn putting out a fire! How can you not see that?" He turns to me with puppy dog eyes. "Bailey, don't you think it looks like a firefighter?"

"I think it's a great rendition of a firefighter," I answer. "You could give Picasso a run for his money."

"Who's Picasso?" Jonah asks.

"He's a famous artist known for his abstract art. Sometimes, you have to dig really deep into your soul to understand some of his work. But when you do, it's eye-opening, and you can't unsee it," I say as tactfully as I can. "I'll show you sometime when there's internet available."

Finn gets to his feet and stretches. He circles to the back side of the couch and leans down so that his breath tickles my ear. Talking softly, he teases, "Nicely done. That was diplomacy at its finest."

"I've had years to master the art," I reply.

When Finn starts putting on his boots, coat, hat, and gloves, Ava hops up and runs over to him. "Where are you going, Finn? Are you gonna play in the snow? Can I come? Please! Please! Please!"

"No, Sweetpea. I've got to shovel the snow, which isn't nearly as much fun. I have to dig a path to the shed to get the snow blower," he tells her.

I walk over and put my hands on Ava's shoulders. "Ava, aren't you going to help us decorate cookies?" I ask, reminding her that we have an indoor task to accomplish.

"We'll get to play in the snow once we get to Pop's and Nana's."

"Okay, Mom. Bye, Finn!" she says, waving as she skips away. Six-year-olds can be easily dissuaded.

"She's cute," Finn says with a slight tilt to his lips.

"She is, and she knows it," I joke. Then my smile slips. "Finn, it's really deep snow out there, and you have less than two hours of light left."

"Are you worried about me, Bailey?" he asks, his voice low and deep.

It seems as though now that the truth is out, Finn has quickly let go of any grudges. I cough and sputter, "I'd be worried about anyone going out in the storm, Finn. It's dangerous, and you're doing this because you *might* get called in. I don't understand why you can't wait until the storm passes or there's a break in the snowfall. I've heard stories of people getting lost ten feet from their homes because they can't see where they're going."

Micah joins me in convincing Finn to wait it out. "Bailey is right. The Chief wouldn't call you in with current visibility and storm conditions, even if you had the ATV or snowmobile ready to go. There's no one out on the roads, and people are tucked safely in their homes. There are enough firefighters and volunteers to assist if there is a problem in town. If the snow stops falling long enough to shovel, I'll be there to help."

"Yeah, stay with us, Finn!" Isaac shouts.

It's not until Jonah says, "We don't want to lose you, too," that Finn finally relents.

Finn takes off his hat and gloves, then slowly removes his coat and boots. "It looks like I'm outnumbered. Bailey, can I have a word with you in private, please?"

I swallow hard and nod. "Ella, do you mind getting started on making some sandwiches for everyone? I know it's late to be eating lunch, but I'm sure we're all a little hungry."

Micah offers to help, which, of course, turns into everyone wanting to make their own sandwich. With Ella and Micah keeping the kids entertained, I follow Finn down the hallway to his bedroom. He gestures for me to sit.

I perch myself on the very edge of the bed so that my toes can touch the floor. "Scold away," I say, joking, even though I'm bracing myself for the worst.

Finn grunts. "I'm not going to scold you, Bailey. You're not a child, and I'll never treat you as one. We've always talked things through, even if it takes us 18 years to do it."

I glance at the floor and make designs on the carpet with my toe. "Then what is it you need to say that couldn't be said in front of the children?"

Finn sits down beside me and clasps his hands together between his knees. "My job is dangerous, and every time I go out on a call, there's a very real possibility that I might not return. It's the main reason I packed up and moved the boys here. If anything were to happen to me, their grandparents would be able to take care of them."

"That makes sense," I say. "Isaac said you moved them here because you needed help."

He bobs his head up and down. "I do, and having my parents close by is a win-win for everyone. The boys get to spend time with their grandparents after school and have a place to stay during my 24-hour shifts. Micah knows the real reason behind our move, but Isaac and Jonah don't."

"Where are you going with this, Finn?"

He takes a deep breath and exhales slowly. "Here's the thing, Bailey. The twins know my job is dangerous, but that isn't what is at the forefront of their minds when I go to work. They wouldn't have thought twice about me shoveling snow in a storm, but because you were worried in front of them, they became worried."

"I'm sorry, Finn. That wasn't my intention, and I completely understand where you're coming from. When we were caught in the snowstorm, I did my best to hide my panic so that the girls wouldn't become scared. I should have been more considerate of you and the boys."

Finn reaches over and grabs my hand, giving it a gentle squeeze. "It's okay, Bailey. Those boys have suffered losses like you wouldn't believe, but they're strong, resilient, and have the most positive outlook on life. I just want to keep that intact as long as possible."

# Chapter Twelve

## Finn

I WALK WITH BAILEY down the hall, and my mouth drops when I see a clean kitchen and six kids munching away on their sandwiches. I turn toward Bailey, "Are you seeing what I'm seeing?"

"Heaven forbid the children are eating without us!" Bailey retorts sarcastically, not comprehending the reason behind my shock or awe. Ella slides over two plates, each containing a sandwich, chips, and a pickle. One plate has a "Bailey-sized" ham sandwich, while the other has a "Finn-sized" turkey sandwich fully loaded with extra meat, cheese, and a third slice of bread.

"It's not that. It's that my kitchen is immaculate! Typically, when the boys are through with anything food-related, it looks like a bomb has gone off in here."

Ella smirks. "Mom taught us to clean as we go. We even used paper plates, so no one has to run a load of dishes."

I narrow my eyes at the three boys staring back at me with pleased expressions. "I've been trying to teach you to do that for months."

"This time, we were motivated," Micah says. So, this is part of their plan to get Bailey on board with giving me a second chance. If she loves them, then she might love me, too. It's false advertising if you ask me, but it just might work. Micah winks for good measure.

"Oh, do you have something stuck in your eye, Micah?" Bailey asks with a motherly concern. I can't hold in my laugh while Micah blushes and focuses on the meal in front of him. I really do have to work with him on his winking technique.

"He's fine," I tell her. Bailey and I thank them for preparing our late lunch and join them at the counter. Bailey picks up the pickle and examines it. "Is there something wrong?" I ask her.

"That's what I'm trying to figure out. The only jar of pickles I saw in the refrigerator ended up shattered on the floor." She bounces the pickle spear at each of the kids in turn. "Are you guys playing a joke on me? Did this come from the trash?"

Ava giggles but shakes her head. "No, Mom. There was another jar in their pantry. The pickles from this morning were on the floor for way more than five seconds."

Mia scrunches her nose in disgust. "The five-second rule is just a myth, Ava. Depending on the type of food, the type of flooring, and the type of bacteria, food can be contaminated instantly. That's why Mom won't let us eat anything that touches the floor. The risk isn't worth the reward."

"It is if I drop my gummy bears," Ava argues back.

The rest of our late lunch is spent talking about our favorite foods, colors, and activities. Bailey listens intently as the boys share since she already knows what her daughters prefer, and I do the same for the girls. "Bailey, if you were stuck on an island and could only have one thing to eat, what would it be?" Isaac asks.

"Mexican food," we say at the same time. I chuckle because Bailey will never pass up the opportunity to eat tacos. Then Bailey glances in my direction and adds, "But sushi comes in a close second. If I was stuck on an island, then I might have to become like Tom Hanks in *Castaway*, spearing fish and eating it raw!"

"Eww! You eat raw fish?" Jonah comments, then makes a gagging motion.

"Not all sushi contains raw fish. But yes, Jonah, I eat it. It's quite delicious when prepared correctly. Have you ever tried it?" Bailey asks him.

Jonah shakes his head adamantly. "No, because it's gross!"

"How do you know if you've never tasted it? You should always try something first before you say you don't like it. It's okay if you don't, but shouldn't that opinion be backed by experience?" Bailey asks him.

Jonah thinks about it for a moment, then nods. "I guess you're right. My mom used to say the same thing about people. She said that we shouldn't dislike someone because we *think* they're not nice or because of someone else's opinion. We should get to know them first and then decide for ourselves."

"Your mom was very wise," Bailey agrees.

When lunch is over, the kids volunteer to clear the plates—which basically means they put them in the trash while I wipe down the counters of the few crumbs that managed to escape. Micah and Ella bring in the first two batches of cookie dough from the back porch, a subtle hint that they're ready to get started on their task.

"Finn, do you have a rolling pin?" Bailey asks as she mixes some powdered sugar and flour together in a bowl.

"My mom had one!" Isaac says and takes off running toward the other end of the house where the boxes of Christmas decorations are stored. Jonah follows him, and together, they bring the large container filled with baking supplies. "We found the cookie cutters in here earlier and a bunch of plastic bags!"

I help the boys unpack the items, and Bailey grins at the piping bags and decorating tips. "I thought I was going to have to go 'old school' and use Ziploc baggies," she says. "I would have cut a tiny hole in the bottom of the bag. It wouldn't have been as pretty, but still a lot of fun."

"You're pretty resourceful, Bailey." I pull out two rolling pins, one ceramic and the other made from wood. Then I frown when I see why the box is so heavy and glance toward Bailey, who is lightly dusting the flour mixture over the countertop.

"What's that look for, Finn?" she asks, tilting her head and narrowing her gaze.

"Please don't hate me," I beg before pulling out a mixer stand. "I had no idea this was in here."

Instead of getting mad that she had to mix everything by hand, Bailey laughs and flexes her tiny bicep. "You got your workout in this morning and so did I," she jokes.

"My muscles are bigger than yours," Jonah says, flexing his bicep as well. "One day, they're going to be as big as Finn's!"

Bailey squeezes Jonah's arm and gasps. "Those are pretty big! You might have even bigger muscles than Finn, especially once you help me roll out the gingerbread. Are you ready to put those bad boys to use?"

Bailey gets the younger kids on task while Ella and Micah assist. Not knowing what to do with myself, I go over and stoke the fire and clean up all the scratch paper from the game earlier. Then I head to my room and dig out my old photo album, dusting off the cover.

I sit in the alcove of the bay window and flip through the pages. The first few are of my family when we lived in California before moving to Lake George before my sophomore year in high school. The pictures feature my sister, Jenny, less and less while Bailey becomes more prominent.

I rub my hand over my favorite picture of Bailey and me after one of my lacrosse games. I'm sweaty and gross, but Bailey still has her arms around my waist and is nuzzling my neck. Her eyes are closed, and her smile reaches from ear to ear. Then I see it.

Daniel is in the background of the picture, but instead of being happy that we won our game, his face is sad as his gaze is locked on Bailey. I flip through more pictures, and most of the time, Daniel has a wistful expression if he's looking at Bailey. If he was looking at me, then his eyes were dark and hollow.

How had I never seen this before? Maybe if I had, I would have questioned Daniel when he lied to me. I pray to God for patience and for the courage to accept that I can't change what happened. But it doesn't stop me from wondering how our lives would have turned out if Bailey and I had gotten married.

I slam the photo album shut when I hear someone coming down the hall. A few seconds later, Bailey appears with a plate of cookies in her hand and knocks on the door frame. "You've been in here for two hours, Finn. What has you so enraptured that even the lure of freshly-baked goods didn't tickle your senses?"

"I was going through an old photo album and stumbled across pictures of you, Daniel, and me. He hated me, Bailey, and I could kick myself for not recognizing it back then."

Bailey sets the plate down on the dresser and sits on the edge of the bed, facing me. "Daniel didn't hate you, Finn."

I open up the album and show her several of the photos. "Look at Daniel in each of these and how he looks at you versus how he looks at me. He's loved you since we were first together, Bailey—not after we graduated, but long before that. Maybe he had his eye on you before I even moved to Lake George. I have to wonder if Daniel was ever my friend or if he just pretended to be so that he could be close to you."

Bailey scrutinizes the images and then shuts the album with a sigh. "It's not hate, Finn. It's jealousy. You had it all. The looks, the talents, the brains, and the girl. From the outside looking in, your life seemed pretty perfect."

It *was* perfect before I mucked everything up because I believed a lie when, in my heart, I should have known the truth. "If it hadn't been for Daniel's lies and deceit, we would have had our 'happily ever after.' I'm trying very hard not to be angry at him."

Bailey stands up and smooths out her reindeer pajama bottoms. "Are you angry at Daniel for lying? Or are you angry at yourself for believing it? Either way, it's anger misspent since there's no way to change the past. You can learn from your mistakes and move on, or you can sit here for another two hours and wallow in self-pity. The choice is yours."

Right before Bailey leaves the room, I ask, "Do you have any regrets, Bailey? Do you regret marrying Daniel after what he did to you and learning what he did to us?"

She shakes her head, loosening a few tendrils from her messy bun. "That's not really a fair question, Finn. I have three reasons in the other room to be thankful for, regardless of the circumstances I find myself in or Daniel's betrayal. They are a blessing and a gift from God. I'm not about to question that gift or the way He provided it. Dwelling on 'what ifs' is a waste of time and energy—energy that I don't have."

Bailey leaves, and I lean my head against the window to stare out at the falling snow. It doesn't appear to be coming down as heavy as it had earlier, but the large flakes are still piling up and lulling me into a trance. I close my eyes as the last vestiges of the sun disappear behind the treetops and cast the forest into shadow.

I feel tiny fingers lift my eyelids, pulling me from my impromptu nap. "Are you sleeping?" Isaac asks with a giggle.

"Not anymore," I say groggily. "What time is it?"

"It's our bedtime," Jonah replies. "You missed all the fun and pizza for dinner. Are you too tired to tuck us in?"

"Nope. I'm never too tired for that. Go and get cleaned up first, then I'll be in to ensure you're snug as a bug." I stretch my arms above my head and roll my neck to work out the kinks. Sleeping while sitting up isn't exactly comfortable, and I envy the rubber necks that children seem to possess.

Isaac shakes his head, and a few droplets of water hit my face. "Bailey already had us take our showers after dinner. I think she's pretty tired, too. You should give her one of your comfy pillows. That will make her fall in love with you."

I pick up the boys and toss them on the bed, eliciting giggles and smiles. I tickle them for good measure. When we're done horsing around, I sit on the edge and lean back. "I want to talk to the two of you for a second. Why do you want to see Bailey and me together? Is it because you miss your mom?"

Both boys are quiet for a few seconds, then Jonah answers. "We miss Mom a whole lot, but what does that have to do with you and Bailey getting married?"

Married? "We aren't at that point, Jonah. Right now, Bailey and I are trying to be friends. I hurt her feelings a long time ago, and it's going to take time to prove to her that I'm sorry. But let's say Bailey and I do decide to pursue a relationship and get married down the road. She would become a mother figure to you. Is that why you want us together?"

Isaac grabs one of my pillows and tucks it under his head as he looks at me. "Bailey is super nice, and she reminds me a lot of Mom. She bakes cookies and loves to cook. She gives good hugs, too, but I don't think she would try to replace Mom."

Jonah bobs his head. "It's just like you, Finn. You aren't our dad, but it doesn't mean you love us any less."

# Chapter Thirteen

## Bailey

Micah and Ella help me clean up the mess from the decorating, and yet we still have four dozen cookies left to finish. It will have to be a project for tomorrow because I'm exhausted and just want to get the scuzz off my body.

"Thanks for the pizza, Bailey," Micah says. "It's the best I've ever had—no lie. Would you be willing to teach me how to make it? I could come to your place for lessons, or better yet, you could come here."

I roll up the wax paper that I used to help protect the counter from dried icing dribbles. "I'd love to. Are you going to have time to learn between school, sports, and your junior firefighting?"

Micah rubs his chin thoughtfully. "Sundays after church would work. All of you could join us for the service, and then we could make the pizzas for lunch afterward. How does that sound?"

Ella balls up the trash bag aprons and tosses them in the garbage. "Please, Mom. It would be fun, and we could make it a standing lunch date."

"I'll think about it. I need to discuss it with Finn first," I tell them both. I look down at my attire and see that my pajama bottoms need a good washing. Most of our clothes are packed up in boxes inside a shipping container being delivered to my parents' house or in our luggage that's still in the food truck. "Ella, can you collect the dirty clothes so I can get a load going in the washer tonight? Set them on the bed, and I'll take care of it."

"I can do the laundry for you, Mom," Ella volunteers. "Mia and Ava are almost ready for bed, and Micah and I were going to stay up and play some video games. It wouldn't be a hardship, and you need your beauty sleep."

I walk around the counter and pull my daughter into an embrace. "A hot shower and sleep sounds good."

"How does a hot bath sound instead?" Finn asks, coming around the corner and holding the plate of cookies

I'd left him. "It's the least I could do since you made me chocolate chip cookies. You know they're my favorite."

The kids all wanted gingerbread or shortbread cookies to decorate, but I snuck in a small batch of chocolate chip for Finn, even though he never spoke up. "I didn't make them for you wanting something in return, Finn."

"I know, and that's why they're special," he retorts. "You're special, Bailey, and you deserve a moment to yourself. The tub is already full, and I set out a pair of sweatpants and a T-shirt on the bed for you. Take all the time you need."

Ella and Micah grin. Ella practically pushes me down the hall toward Finn's room and the master bath. "Mom, Finn is trying to do something nice for you. You deserve to be pampered. Enjoy the moment, and when you're done, say 'Thank you' and give Finn a big kiss."

I walk into Finn's room, and just before I shut and lock the door, what she said registers in my brain. "Ella, what's going on?"

Ella shrugs. "Mom, Mia, Ava, and I just want you to be happy. Finn made you happy once. Maybe if you give him a chance, he can do it again."

"You've known him less than two days, Ella."

"True," she says. "But if Dad hadn't lied to Finn and manipulated you, then you and Finn would be together. You are meant to be together. I can tell."

I open my mouth to argue and give her my little spiel, but she raises a hand to stop me. "I know what you're going to say, Mom. You're going to tell me that you wouldn't want to change the past because then you wouldn't have us. And that's the thing; you don't have to. You can still have a future with Finn, and us girls will be the gift that keeps on giving," she winks.

"What about Mia and Ava? Aren't they going to think I'm trying to replace their father if I start dating Finn? That's assuming that Finn wants to date me."

Ella grabs my hands and uses the 'mom' tone against me, her face serious and stern. "Dad can be as much of a participant in our lives as he wants to be; which for the past few years hasn't been much. I pray every day that changes, but it's up to him to get things figured out. I don't think, for even two seconds, that Finn would stand in the way of whatever relationship Dad has with us. But Mia and Ava need a positive male role model in their lives, and as much as I don't want to say it, Dad isn't it—not as things currently stand."

"So, if your dad were to show up tomorrow and beg for a second chance, you don't think Mia and Ava would want me to take it?" I ask, testing the water.

Ella shakes her head vehemently. "Not if it means that you're unhappy, Mom. Dad made his choice, and it wasn't us. Even at six years old, Ava recognizes this. Finn made a mistake years ago that cost you both dearly, but everything happens for a reason. You taught us that. Maybe the reason our gas gauge got stuck and we were rescued by Finn is God's handiwork at play."

"You're going to make a wonderful mother someday, Ella. You're wise beyond your years."

Ella laughs. "I hope so, but not for a long time yet. Go and enjoy the bath before the water gets cold, and think about what I said, okay?"

I hug my daughter. "Okay. I'll think about it, but I make no promises."

I shut the door and flip the lock, heading for the bathroom. My eyes well with tears when I see all the trouble Finn has gone through to provide a relaxing experience for me. The sunken bathtub is filled with warm water and bubbles, along with a large candle flickering in the corner.

I'm about to strip off my flour-crusted clothing when there's a knock at the door. "Bailey, are you still decent?" Finn asks.

I open his bedroom door and let him in. "Only if you consider puffy eyes and filthy clothes decent."

Finn steps inside, holding a chilled glass of white wine. He notices my red-rimmed eyes and wipes away the lone tear on my cheek with the pad of his thumb. "Bailey Bug, why are you crying?"

"They're happy tears, Finn. I promise." I wave my hand toward the open bathroom door. "I'm a little overwhelmed by the sweet gesture. That's all. It's been so long since someone has gone out of their way for me—my girls excluded, of course."

"You deserve to be treated like a queen, Bailey. I'm sorry that hasn't been the case. What you did for the boys today meant something to them, and it meant something to me. This is my way of saying thank you. Here," Finn says, handing me the glass of wine. "Relax and unwind. I'll finish cleaning up in the kitchen."

I take the offered glass and step back because if I don't, I might end up kissing Finn as Ella had suggested. I might, anyway, because he's standing there with a vulnerable expression. "Thank you. You didn't have to do this, but I really appreciate it."

"It's my pleasure." As Finn closes the door, I hear him mumble, "I'd do anything for you."

I lock the door behind him, not entirely sure I was supposed to hear that last part. Finn had always treated me with respect and love, which is why his ghosting me broke my heart.

I set the glass down on the edge of the tub while I undress and slip into the warm water topped with bubbles. The fruity scent tickles my nose as I lean my head back and close my eyes. I briefly wonder why Finn has bubble bath to begin with, but I let the thought go. It's none of my business.

If Finn wants a second chance with me, would it be wise to give it to him? Could I trust him not to break my heart a second time if I did? Heck, I don't know if I'm ready to put myself out there again, not so soon after my divorce.

After an hour of contemplation and a second warm-up to the bath water, I still don't have the answers to the questions bouncing around in my head. I decide to "Let go and let God" because my head and heart are warring against one another. My head is blaring a warning that I should protect myself from ever being hurt again while my heart remembers the way it beat rapidly whenever Finn held me in his arms.

I let the water drain as I drip dry and search for a towel. I find them stashed under the bathroom sink along with the bottles of bubble bath. I laugh when I read the label out loud. "Children's fruit-scented bubble bath. Non-toxic and gentle on the skin." The name Jonah is scrawled on the label. There's another bottle next to it with the name Isaac scrawled across the top. Apparently, Isaac prefers bubble-gum-scented bubble baths instead of smelling like a fruit salad.

I'm grateful to Finn for leaving me clean, warm clothes to wear, but Finn is nearly twice my size, and they don't quite fit as intended. When I put on the sweatpants, the waistband is at my armpits, and I giggle as the image of Steve Urkel pops into my head. I roll up the cuffs and roll down the waistband until the sweats fit my tiny frame. The T-shirt hangs to mid-thigh and swims on me, yet I can't take my eyes off my reflection in the mirror. The shirt is

Finn's Lake George Leopards tee, and the name Hollister is displayed prominently across my shoulders.

I gather up the extra material and tie a knot at the front, keeping the shirt a little loose but not wearing it like a dress. I blow out the candle and clean up the bathroom, gathering up my dirty clothes and the towel I used.

Walking down the hall, I hear Finn talking with Ella and Micah and stop in my tracks. "Your mom was the best thing that ever happened to me. I was a fool for letting her go."

Micah pipes up and says, "But she loved you so much. I don't understand how you could leave her like that?"

"Fear," Finn says bluntly.

Micah scoffs. "But you're the bravest person I know. You literally jump out of planes with nothing more than a handful of tools to put out forest fires. You laugh in the face of danger."

Finn chuckles, but there's no mirth in it. "Fear of rejection, Micah. I know it sounds ridiculous, but it's true."

"Do you still miss her? Do you still love her?" Ella asks, sounding forlorn and heartbroken.

I frown. Finn seems to have a penchant for loving and leaving not only me, but Micah's mom as well. I back up slowly so as not to draw attention to myself, but that doesn't stop me from overhearing his choked-out response. "I miss her every day, Ella. She was my world, and

I'll always love her. There isn't a day that goes by I haven't thought about her."

I finally make it back to Finn's room and softly close the door, allowing my back to slide down the wood until my but hits the floor. Touching my forehead to my knees, I begin to let the tears flow. How could I be so naïve?

## Chapter Fourteen

### Finn

I KEEP GLANCING IN the direction of the hallway, hoping that Bailey will come out and join us. Telling two teenagers how much I've missed Bailey and that leaving her was the worst mistake I ever made isn't exactly how I planned on spending my evening. My only hope is that they can learn something from my experience.

Ella gives me a hug. "Finn, I know my mom better than anyone. I'm practically her 'mini-me.' I know how she thinks and how she operates. If you really want to pick up where you left off, then you are going to have to show her you are in it to win it."

"Bailey isn't a prize, and I don't want to pick up where we left off," I tell Ella. My eyes dart between both of the teens as I explain, "If Bailey is willing to give me a second chance, then I want to start over and create something new. Life has changed and shaped us into who we are today, which isn't two teenagers ignorant of the world around them. If Bailey and I decide to date one another, then we are going to have to get to know each other all over again."

Micah grins from his perch on the recliner. "You're such a sap, Finn. It's cute."

Ella giggles. "Micah, we use the term 'cinnamon roll' when it comes to people like Finn. It means they're all ooey-gooey and sicky sweet."

I lift one shoulder. "Ella, your mom deserves sweet. She always has."

Ella's smile turns upside down. "My dad wasn't really the 'sweet' kind of guy." When Ella sees my scowl in response, she raises her hands to placate me. "He wasn't mean or anything, Finn. He just didn't give out hugs freely or say 'I love you' nearly enough. I don't ever recall my dad bringing home flowers for mom 'just because' or even chocolate on Valentine's Day. You did more for her in the last 24 hours than my dad has done in the last 24 months. I bet Mom cried when you made her a hot bath."

I don't confirm or deny Ella's assertion. I glance down the hall, getting worried that Bailey may have fallen asleep in the tub. It's been nearly two hours. "Ella, can you go check on your mom? I know I told her to take all the time she needs, but..."

"Sure." Ella leaves and returns less than a minute later with a pile of dirty clothes in her hand. "Um, Finn? Do you have somewhere else you can sleep tonight?"

My eyebrow arches up, and I look at Ella with a perplexed expression. "Why?"

Ella glances over her shoulder down the hall. "My mom must have thought your bed was more comfortable than Micah's because she's fast asleep. Trying to wake her is like trying to wake the dead."

I rub my face and glance over at Micah. He points at me and says, "You've already relegated me to the couch. If you want to sleep out here, you get the recliner. This way, your head is in an upright position, and I don't have to listen to you snore."

"I don't snore," I argue.

Ella cocks her hip and her head. "How would you know?"

"You totally snore, Finn," Micah says adamantly. "It's so bad that I think you should get tested for sleep apnea. Then you can look like Mr. Snuffleupagus and sound like Darth Vader." He makes the Darth Vader breathing sounds and then mimics, "Luuuke...I am your fah-tha."

I throw a couch pillow at his head as I get up to grab a change of clothes and an extra blanket. "You are definitely your mother's child."

I tiptoe down the hallway, praying I don't wake Bailey up with the creak of the floorboards. When I enter the room, Bailey is right where Ella warned me that she would be. Bailey is curled up on my bed with her hands tucked up under her cheek. I gently tuck a wisp of hair behind her ear and kiss her temple. I whisper, "Sleep well, my fair princess."

·♥·♥·♥·♥·♥·

Early the next morning, I briefly stir when a warm body curls up beside me on the recliner. Ava nestles in next to me and makes herself at home. Without a moment's thought, I cover her with a blanket before wrapping my arms around her and tucking her head under my chin. I fall back asleep only to wake up to eyes boring into me like laser beams.

Bailey stands over me with her hands on her hips. She whispers so as not to wake Ava or Micah, "What are you doing, Finn?"

"Sleeping. At least, I was trying to."

"I meant, why is my daughter cuddled up next to you?" she asks.

I close my eyes and turn my head away. "Ask her when she wakes up. What time is it, anyway?"

"It's almost five," Bailey retorts.

I groan. "Give me another hour, please. I need my handsome sleep."

"Handsome sleep? What the heck is that?"

Micah pulls a sofa pillow over his head. "It's the male version of 'beauty sleep.' I'd like to get some, too, if you don't mind."

"Sorry, Micah," Bailey whispers. Then she turns to me, "We will talk about this later."

Half an hour later and unable to go back to sleep, I scoot out from underneath Ava and leave her curled up peacefully on the recliner. I check both Micah's room and mine, looking for Bailey, but she's not there.

I head to the basement and find her bent over the washing machine with her feet kicking wildly in the air as she digs out the remaining few socks that are stuck on the bottom. She grumbles, "Why couldn't Finn have a front loader? Doesn't he realize that some of us are vertically challenged and not everyone is as tall and beefy as he is?"

I chuckle. "There's a step stool next to the washer, Bailey."

"Oh, Finn. You're up," she says, blowing away the loose tendrils of blonde hair that have fallen in her face.

"It was hard to go back to sleep after your 5:00 a.m. wake-up call. Usually, if I'm woken up at that hour, it's to a fire alarm or medical emergency. What was your emergency that we need to discuss?"

She throws the last few articles of clothing into the dryer and turns it on before jumping up and planting her butt on top. "I wanted to talk to you about Ava snuggling up with you and what it means."

I fold my arms across my chest and lean my back against the wall. "And what does it mean, Bailey?"

"Ava doesn't snuggle up with just anyone, Finn. She snuggles up with people she *loves* and trusts."

"I'm trying to see how that's a problem, Bailey. Isn't it a good thing that Ava doesn't think I'm a serial killer? Although I have been known to destroy a box of Cocoa Puffs in one sitting."

Bailey huffs. "This isn't a joke, Finn. It's been two days, and Ava is already getting attached to you."

"How is that bad, Bailey? It's a small town, and having people who adore her is a positive in my book. Having people in her corner is always a good thing."

"Until they're not! Then her heart will be broken because she won't understand why she was abandoned, and she'll spend years questioning her own self-worth, Finn."

I move slowly from my perch on the wall and stalk toward Bailey, who, by the way, looks adorable in my shirt and sweatpants. I cage her in and invade her comfort bubble, placing a hand on each side of her. My voice deepens when I confront the truth of what she's trying to say.

"This isn't about Ava, is it? I think you're getting attached to me, and that scares you."

Bailey lowers her eyes and stares at her dangling feet. "It terrifies me, Finn. When I decided to move back here with the girls, I wasn't given any warning that you had returned. If I had, I may have chosen to start over somewhere else. Forgiving you doesn't mean I can forget what happened between us. *Gah!* Loving you was so easy, but getting over you was the hardest thing I have ever had to do. It's why Daniel and I moved away. He knew that everywhere was a reminder of what you and I had shared."

I tuck a strand of hair behind Bailey's ear and stroke her cheek gently with my calloused thumb. "I'm not going anywhere, Bailey. You don't have to worry about me abandoning you or the girls. You don't have to question your self-worth, and I'm truly sorry that my actions caused you ever to do that in the first place. If you give me the chance, I'll prove it to you. I'll prove that you are worth walking through fire for."

Bailey puts her hand on my heart and subtly shakes her head. "You've made those promises to me before. Did you make the same promises to Micah's, Isaac's, and Jonah's mother?"

"What?"

"I overheard your conversation last night with Ella and Micah. You told Micah that you left his mother for fear of rejection but that you still love her and miss her every day," Bailey says. "For Pete's sake, the boys call you 'Finn' and not 'Dad.'"

I palm my face as I think about all the conversations about the boys' mother since we rescued Bailey and the girls from the snowstorm. Not once did Jenny's name come up. I just assumed that Bailey knew who their mother was. I start cackling uncontrollably at the absurdity of this whole situation. "You have…it…so wrong…Bailey," I say, doubled over in amusement.

I wipe the tears from my eyes and regain a modicum of control. "If anyone would find humor in this situation, it would be the boys' mother. Micah, Isaac, and Jonah are my nephews—not my children, Bailey. After their father died six years ago fighting a fire, Jenny changed her will to make me their guardian should anything happen to her."

It hits her that it's my sister who passed away. "I'm so sorry, Finn. I had no idea that Jenny was their mom or that she passed away. Micah is the spitting image of you, and I assumed…."

The smile disappears from my face in an instant. "You assumed that I would abandon my family as I had you, and I didn't give you any reason to believe otherwise. But that's not who I am, Bailey. I'm as committed as they come, which is why I haven't loved anyone else. You've always been it for me."

"What are you saying, Finn?"

I lean forward and brush my lips against hers in a soft but chaste kiss. But once I've had a taste, there is no going back. I press my lips firmly to hers as my fingers grip the dryer rather than roam her body like I want to. She tilts her head and invites me in by parting her lips slightly before her hand slides around my neck as she deepens the kiss even further. When her ankle slides around my calf, I realize that we are getting carried away and pull back. I need to lay all my cards on the table so that she knows exactly where I stand.

"I've never stopped loving you, Bailey Bug," I say, nipping at her bottom lip. "You've always been my forever, even if you gave up believing I'm yours."

# Chapter Fifteen

## Bailey

*"I'VE NEVER STOPPED LOVING you, Bailey Bug. You've always been my forever, even if you gave up believing I'm yours."*

I feel like such a schmuck for making the same mistake Finn did all those years ago and believing the worst without having all the facts. I'm really glad it didn't take us another 18 years before the truth came out, but I'm not sure I'm ready to process what Finn just said or that fact he pulled away. It's for the best because, for a minute, I lost myself in his kiss.

The sweet feel of Finn's lips against mine makes me want to throw all caution out the window and leap without a parachute, but I still have three girls to think about and a shipping container of boxes to unpack. I have a business I need to get off the ground, and yet I don't even have a home that I can call my own. I'm feeling adrift in a sea of overwhelming emotions, tasks, and responsibilities with nothing but Ava's arm floaties to keep me from sinking.

"Finn, what am I supposed to say to that?"

He pushes off the washer and takes a step back. "I don't expect you to say anything, Bailey. I simply thought you should know how I feel about you—how I've always felt about you."

"We can't simply pick up where we left off, Finn. There's too much history, and we aren't the same people anymore," I tell him. Although the idea of rekindling our relationship is becoming more appealing with every subtle hint he drops.

Finn makes his way over to the stairs and leans on the railing. "You're right, but that doesn't mean we can't wipe the slate clean and start over. If I could have one thing for Christmas, I'd ask for a second chance. But if you're not ready or that's not what you want, then I'd rather have your friendship than nothing at all. How about we start there? If, or when, you decide you want more, I'll be waiting with arms wide open. I've waited 18 years to make things right. I can wait as long as you need."

I hop off the dryer, my butt having gone numb due to the constant vibration. "Be honest with me, Finn. Are you really okay with being just friends if that's what I decide, even after our shared history? Do you believe it's possible to be only friends because that's where I'd like to start for now?"

"It's not what I want, but I'll take what I can get, Bailey. If it means you and the girls get to be a part of our lives, then yes, I'm okay with being friends. The question is, are you?" He pounds the banister twice with his fist to end the conversation and heads upstairs.

I check the timer on the dryer and note that there's half an hour left on the cycle before I go trudging up the stairs. I make my way to the kitchen, where Finn has a steaming cup of coffee waiting for me. "You really are a hero," I whisper, taking the mug from his hands. "Thank you."

He chuckles. "You don't have to whisper. The kids most likely won't be up for another couple of hours, and Micah moved to my room so that we didn't have to tiptoe around. Ava is out like a light and still asleep on the recliner."

I smile and blow on the coffee. "She can sleep through a hurricane."

Finn leans casually against the counter. "Did you get a lot of those?"

"Hurricanes? A few, but most of them were storms by the time they hit our area. Hurricane Sandy was the worst, but we evacuated for that one. We lived far enough inland that the flooding didn't affect our home. The restaurant, on the other hand, took almost a month to clean up and most of our savings to get operational. It was another year before we were back in the black."

"What was the name of your restaurant?" Finn asks.

"Eclecticity."

Deep lines form between Finn's eyes as he digests the name, no pun intended. "Interesting name for a restaurant. Although I wouldn't know what kind of food you served with a name like that."

"That's the point, but Daniel thought it was a dumb name, too, and we fought for months over it. I had just graduated from culinary school and loved to make all kinds of ethnic foods. As you know, Mexican food is my favorite, but I also love the rich spices of Indian food. Then there's Southern comfort food, Asian fusion, Italian, and French. The list goes on and on and I couldn't decide. I wanted to do them all, and so I did."

"How?" Finn asks, genuinely curious how I could accomplish such a feat.

"Every month, we featured a new cuisine. Man, you should have seen the spice pantry. If a spice existed, we had it."

Finn pours himself a glass of milk and unwraps the plate of chocolate chip cookies. There's significantly less on the plate than when I gave it to him yesterday. "That name makes perfect sense with your menu. I think it's great. Are you planning on doing something like that in Lake George?"

I grab one of the cookies and dunk it in my coffee. "Probably not. Running a restaurant of that magnitude took up so much of my time and energy. Even though I loved it, I love my girls more. I want to be able to spend time with them before it's too late. I have my food truck for festivals and concert venues, but I was thinking of opening up a small bakery once I get the proceeds from the sale of the house."

Finn dunks a cookie in his glass of milk, and his eyes roll back in his head as he savors the treat. "Best bweakfast evah!" he says with his mouth full. He finishes chewing and swallows before asking me, "If you started a bakery—which is an amazing idea, by the way—what would you call it?"

"You're going to think it's silly," I say with downcast eyes. Daniel never liked my creative spin on anything but usually gave up the fight since he wasn't the one making the dishes or doing the actual work in the kitchen. He managed the books because he excelled at numbers.

Finn sets down his glass and lifts my chin so that I can see his earnest expression. "It's okay to be silly. It's your shop. It's your choice. Please tell me. I promise I won't laugh."

I mumble, "Baileys and Buttercream."

"That's a perfect name for a bakery, Bailey. Can I assume that buttercream icing will be a staple? I beg you to make it a staple because if you do, you have at least one customer for life," Finn asks, his eyes sparkling with delight. I perfected my buttercream icing years ago because that was Finn's favorite, and he has always wanted it on his birthday cakes. Even my pastry arts teacher raved about it.

"It might be," I tease. "Enough about me. I want to hear about your adventures. I bet smoke jumping was exciting and dangerous."

"It wasn't like I moved to California and went right into jumping out of airplanes. I served as a firefighter for Lake Tahoe for ten years before I was trained as a smoke jumper. I've broken my leg twice when the winds shifted and have ended up landing in a tree on more than one occasion."

I gasp. "Oh, no! Was that the worst injury you ever had?"

He shakes his head and pulls up his pant leg. "You'll almost never see me wear shorts because of this." Underneath his sweatpants is a mass of scar tissue from a severe burn. "It took several skin grafts to make it look this sexy."

I reach out and touch it lightly. "Does it still hurt?"

He chuckles. "It hurt like the dickens when it happened six years ago, but I don't feel anything there now. You could poke me with a needle, and I wouldn't feel it."

"What happened?" I ask.

Finn's face falls. "We were fighting a fire at an abandoned lodge. A couple of kids thought it would be cool to camp out in the vacant building, but their campfire got out of control. They were trapped, and our team went in to rescue them. Jenny's husband and the boys' father, Josiah, was with me when a beam collapsed and fell on us both. I was able to get out from underneath the beam, but Josiah was knocked out cold. I had a choice to make. Save the kids or save Josiah. I couldn't do both."

I set my coffee cup down and wrap my arms around his waist, letting his tears fall on me as he embraces me back. He continues his story. "I thought that Jenny and the kids would hate me and blame me for his death once they found out. But they didn't. Jenny said that Josiah would have done the same thing if the roles had been reversed. Josiah knew the risks. They all did. Jenny lost her husband, and the boys lost their father, and I got a constant reminder of my failure."

I run my finger down Finn's cheek and kiss the corner of his mouth. "You didn't fail, Finn. I didn't know Josiah, but if he loved firefighting as much as you do, then he died doing what he loved. Two lives were saved because of his actions and yours. Maybe those kids will go on to do something that will save countless more lives. You never know what God's plan is."

Finn releases me, so I let my arms drop down by my side. "Thanks, Bailey. When I said that Micah, Isaac, and Jonah had seen loss, now you know what I meant. Then Jenny died last year after getting really sick. I have contemplated giving up being a firefighter so that they don't have to endure any more loss."

Micah walks in at that moment and heads straight for the coffee pot. He reaches for a mug and sets it on the counter before turning and facing Finn. "Loss is a part of life, Finn. If you give up what you love most, then a piece of you will die inside. You won't be Finn anymore, but rather a shell of the man we know, love, and respect."

Finn brushes past me to place a hand on Micah's shoulder. He looks the young teen squarely in the eyes. "I'd give up everything because I love you more."

Micah hugs Finn and says, "I know you would, but we love you enough that we would never ask you to."

They hold their embrace until Micah pushes away. "So enough mushy stuff. What's for breakfast?"

"Oatmeal," I tease. "I'm in the mood for mushy."

Micah groans. "Oatmeal is boring. It's like eating flavorless boogers."

Finn barks out a laugh. "And what is a booger supposed to taste like, Micah? Do tell!"

Micah blushes. "I'll rephrase. I *imagine* it's like eating flavorless boogers."

Mia walks in wearing her flannel jammies. "There are booger-flavored jellybeans. There are even ones that taste like dirt and earwax. Maybe you should ask whoever created those how *they* know what a booger tastes like."

"Thanks, Mia, for the lesson on flavor profiles. How about we change the subject?" I suggest, getting a little grossed out by the topic of conversation. "I was thinking about making French toast eggs-in-a-hole."

Ava peeks her head over the back of the recliner, her blond hair a matted mess and a crust of drool down her chin. "I want my hole to be a snowflake!"

Mia turns to her sister. "Then it's not a hole, Ava. It's eggs-in-a-snowflake."

Ava scowls and sticks out her tongue. "I. Don't. Care. Mia. Potato—Tomato."

Mia opens her mouth to correct Ava, and I stop her before this has a chance to devolve into a full-blown argument. "You both know the rule. Two cups of coffee, then it's fair game. I'll make the second cup last until well past noon if you can't rein it in."

I pull out a bowl and another two dozen eggs. I whip up a French toast mixture with cinnamon, vanilla, and a hint of maple syrup stirred in. Isaac and Jonah make their way downstairs as if they know breakfast is about to be made.

Since my daughters already know how to make this dish, I teach Isaac and Jonah how to make eggs-in-a-hole, except the toast will be French toast. Micah watches intently and absorbs information like a sponge. I take a loaf of bread and set them out on a sheet of wax paper and then lay out the various cookie cutters. "You can use any cookie cutter available as long as it fits inside the crust of the bread. It's important to keep the crust intact."

By the time I have breakfast made, there are every manner of Christmas shapes. There are snowflakes, gingerbread men, snowmen, Christmas trees, stars, candy canes, stockings, and mittens.

Finn looks at the plates and chortles. "At least no one will argue about whose is whose."

We all take our plates and sit at the dining room table, which Ella and Micah have set with condiments and glasses of juice. Finn says grace. "Heavenly Father, thank You for Your provisions and for gathering us all here together. We thank You for providing us shelter, not only with a roof over our heads but with Your protection during this storm. We thank you for the hands that have prepared this food and for family and friendships, new, old, and renewed. Your grace is sufficient, and Your mercy endures forever. Your love is unconditional and unfailing. In Your name, we pray, Amen."

"Amen."

# Chapter Sixteen

## Finn

Tomorrow is Christmas Eve, and Micah hands everyone an envelope, a piece of paper, and a pen. "This is something our mom started when I was just a small child, but it's grown into a tradition our family has adopted over the years," Micah says. "This is just a simple request to God for one intangible thing. In essence, it's a prayer that's short and sweet. Tomorrow morning, we'll open them up and read them aloud so that God hears our prayers."

Micah faces Mia and directs his next comment at her because she's always quick to correct and impart her vast knowledge to those around her. She's 10 going on 60, and Micah has already recognized this in the short time he's known her. "I know that God knows our hearts and thoughts, Mia, but Matthew 18:20 states, 'For where two or three are gathered in my name, there am I among them.' When we read these prayers aloud, we want Jesus present with us because we're all together."

Mia doesn't argue and even gives Micah a genuine smile. Everyone nods their heads in agreement, and Ava immediately starts scribbling on her paper. Bailey stands up and hugs Micah. "This is something that's special for you and your family. Thank you for allowing us to share in this moment."

"You can be part of our family, Bailey," Isaac informs her. "I like Ella and Ava because they're sweet."

"I like Mia because she puts Isaac in his place," Jonah adds. "She can stay and be my friend."

Mia throws her arm around Jonah. "I knew I liked you for a reason."

Isaac laughs. "Seriously, Bailey. We love you all."

"How about we write our letters now," I interject, hoping that Bailey won't become uncomfortable by the invite into our family. She and I are still trying to find our footing as friends.

We each write our letters, and I can't help but laugh at Ava, who is the last to finish. Her little tongue is sticking out of the corner of her mouth, and there are drawings all over the page. She hands Bailey the letter to fold and put in the envelope. "You can't look, Mom. It's between me and God."

"God and me," Mia corrects. Bailey glares at Mia, and Mia glares back. "What? Are you upset because I beat you to it?"

Bailey sighs and smirks. "A little."

Bailey looks away as she folds the paper for Ava, and Ava shouts, "You're messing up my prayer! Now, it's all crooked!"

Bailey slides the paper over to Ava, who gladly takes it back and then folds it nearly a thousand times until it's a tiny square instead of the trifold the rest of us have done. Her little nugget of paper is going to take until Christmas to unfold. She drops it in the envelope and seals it shut.

For the next few hours, Bailey and the kids have a ton of fun as they finish decorating the rest of the cookies. I sit on the couch and watch how they all interact. Isaac and Jonah are hanging on Bailey's every word, but Micah is leaning on the counter, watching them just as I am. He winks at me and gives me a thumbs-up behind Bailey's back.

Ella walks over to the window and says absentmindedly, "The snow has stopped falling."

That's my cue to get up and start shoveling. "Micah, I need you to help me dig a path to the shed and the garage. We need to get the ATVs and snowmobiles free and clear, ready to use."

Ava frowns and starts to sniffle. "Is it already time for us to leave? I like it here."

Bailey consoles her daughter. "Pops and Nana are waiting for us. All your Christmas presents are under their tree."

"I don't care about the presents. I want to stay here and play Pictionary," Ava wails. "Jonah is so bad at drawing; I can actually win!"

Jonah's eyebrows furrow. "I'm the next Picasso, Ava. My art just needs to be understood."

I start laughing and then notice Ella and Micah sneak away into the dining room. Bailey is too busy wrangling the kids to see what's happening, so I get up and approach the teens stealthily and hide behind the French doors.

"You know what you have to do, Micah," Ella says with a conspiratorial tone.

"I'll do what I can if I get the chance. You can count on me," Micah replies. "We don't have much time. Did you find what you were looking for?"

Ella huffs. "Not exactly, but it will do in a pinch."

· ♥ · ♥ · ♥ · ♥ · ♥ ·

An hour later, Micah and I are wearing snowshoes so we can traverse the ten feet of snow that has fallen. I plant my shovel in the snow and stand with my hands on my hips, scanning the area. "The shed has got to be around here somewhere. We have to be getting close since the garage is right there," I say, pointing to the structure to our two o'clock position.

Micah laughs. "It's only the top five feet of the garage. There's so much snow that the shed has completely disappeared! Finn, I know you don't want to hear it, but you might have to concede defeat."

"I can't do that, Micah. Christmas is two days away, and we need to get Bailey and the girls to their family." I pick up my shovel and start pile-driving it into the snow, hoping at some point I'll make contact with the roof of the shed. Two minutes later, I hit pay dirt. "Here it is!"

It takes Micah and me nearly two hours to dig our way to the door. We create a "snow" ramp on the side of the shed so we can get the snowblower out. Although it's nearly freezing outside, I'm dripping with sweat from the exertion. "At least the hard part is done. Now comes the fun part!"

"You really need to get out more if you think shoveling anything is fun," Micah retorts.

"It's character building. And if manual labor isn't your thing, then you can consider it exercise. We didn't get gym time this morning, and now we can count this as our full-body workout!"

"I have enough character," he says. "Let's see how much we can get done. I'm missing out on decorating the last of the cookies. I take my job as 'Quality Control Specialist' very seriously."

I laugh and fire up the motor. "At least you take *something* seriously."

Six hours and two breaks later, we've accomplished the task of digging a path to the garage that's wide enough to drive the ATVs outside and park them under the balcony on the back side of the house. There's about six feet between the top of the snow and the bottom of the deck. We finish just as the sun makes its final descent.

Micah pulls off his hat, and his head is soaking wet. "I need a hot shower and some dry clothes."

"You and me, both." I slide open the window and allow Micah to crawl through first before I follow. As we sit on the floor and take off our snowshoes, I say, "We don't have much time to take the girls into town. Another storm is heading our way, and I don't know how long it will be before it gets here."

Micah heads into the attached bathroom to remove the snowsuit so that he doesn't make a mess on the carpet. I do the same. As he sits on the edge of the bathtub to remove his boots, he says, "It's too late to take them tonight. We should wait until tomorrow—for safety's sake."

"You just want them to stay. Micah. I know that having them here has been fun, but it's not going to be the last we're ever going to see of them."

"Does that mean that you and Bailey are a couple now?" he asks, his tone hopeful and his eyes shimmering with joy.

"We decided to be friends for now, and I'm honestly surprised she's willing to do that after how I treated her years ago." I gather up our snowsuits and head downstairs.

Micah chases after me and stops me at the edge of the landing. He lowers his voice, "But you want more, right?"

I nod. "I've told Bailey that I'll wait until she's ready. She has a lot on her plate right now, and she needs a friend more than she needs a romantic relationship. The ball is in her court. She knows where I stand."

Micah rests his hand on my shoulder. "Finn. Finn. Finn. You're going to get friend-zoned if you go in with that attitude. You need to give her a taste of what she'll be missing out on. Have you kissed her yet?"

I'm not about to divulge any details about our kiss in the basement, but it was enough for Bailey to understand that my feelings for her aren't purely platonic. "Yes, but that doesn't change the circumstances."

Micah rubs his chin thoughtfully. "Hmm."

"'Hmm,' nothing, Micah. You got your wish and brought Bailey and me together, even if it wasn't how you expected. Let's leave well enough alone and let the relationship progress naturally. If it's meant to be more, then it will be. Now, go get a shower, and then meet me downstairs."

As we amble down the steps, Micah grumbles, "Sometimes even nature needs a helping hand."

I let the comment go and continue toward the mudroom in the basement, having to pass by the kitchen on my way. Bailey smiles, and her shoulders slump in relief when she sees me. "I was starting to get worried about you two. You guys were out there a long time."

"There was a ton of snow to clear, and even then, we only managed to clear enough to get the ATVs. Thankfully, I had already installed the snow track conversion kits. Otherwise, I'd still be out there for another few hours. They're parked out back under the balcony."

Bailey walks over to one of the windows facing the back of the house, and she grimaces. "Are you planning on taking us to town tonight?"

When Micah mentioned that it wouldn't be safe to travel tonight, he wasn't wrong. However, I knew that his motivation for not leaving right away had nothing to do with safety and everything to do with keeping Bailey and the girls here a little longer. "We can if you absolutely need to go, but tomorrow after breakfast would be better. My only concern is not knowing how much of a lull we have between storms."

She wraps her arms around her delicate frame and slowly heads in my direction. "It's a concern of mine as well, and I know my parents are giddy with excitement for our pending arrival. They haven't seen the girls in over a year. However, I like the idea of waiting until morning when everyone is well-rested, fed, and can see where they're going. It'll give me the warm fuzzies."

"I like warm fuzzies," Jonah says. "They keep my toes from getting cold. Besides, you can't leave until we open up the envelopes."

Bailey gives him a noogie on his noggin. "We wouldn't miss it for the world. Jesus is the reason for the season, after all, and I absolutely love that you write letters to Him instead of Santa."

Isaac's upper lip curls. "My mom would say that 'Jesus is the reason for *every* season.' She never taught us to believe in Santa Claus. Bailey, do you believe in Santa?"

"I don't, but I used to when I was Ava's age," she admits. "It was very disappointing to learn that Santa isn't real. It's why I never taught my girls to believe in him. I wanted them to know that I would always tell them the truth, no matter what."

Jonah grins. "Our mom said the same thing. If she taught us to believe in Jesus and Santa, and then we learn Santa isn't real, she was afraid we would question if Jesus was real, too."

I dip my chin toward the pile of snowsuits in my hand that are getting heavy. "I'm going to hang these up to dry and then warm up with a quick shower." Bailey waves me away as she continues her engaging conversation with the twins.

While downstairs in the basement area, I reflect on a conversation between Jenny and Bailey when my sister was home from college for the holiday break in my senior year. They discussed the merits of whether or not teaching kids to believe in Santa was a good or bad thing. I remember my sister saying, *"I don't begrudge the families that teach their kids about Santa Claus—to each their own. Personally, I don't want to deal with the fallout, and I don't think it's going to ruin the holiday if my children don't believe in a mythical being."*

Bailey had asked her, *"Then how will you explain why there are presents under the tree?"*

Jenny had laughed. *"That's easy. What do you give when it's someone's birthday? A present, right? I'll just tell my kids that we exchange presents because it's a party for Jesus' birthday. Look, Bailey. When you and Finn get married and have kids of your own, it will be up to the two of you to decide what to teach your kids and what you want them to believe in. Regardless of what you decide, I'll still love you."*

It's evident that my sister had an impact on Bailey, considering that Bailey took her advice to heart. Jenny loved Bailey like a sister and had urged me to fight for her. Jenny hadn't believed for one second that Bailey had betrayed me but respected me enough to refrain from discussing or pursuing it any further. It wasn't until Jenny was near her end that she finally spoke up.

*"Finn, you know I love you, right?"* I held her hand and nodded, waiting for her to continue. Whenever she started off a sentence with that particular question, what she liked to call 'constructive criticism' often followed. *"You have spent your entire adult life pining after Bailey because you let pride get in your way. I know that you still love her, but brother of mine, you need to make things right so that you can move on. You need closure."*

*"Bailey is happy, and the last thing I want to do is drudge up the past, Jenny,"*

Jenny laughed and then groaned in pain because her Leukemia made it painful to breathe. *"I'm happy when I have a scoop of salted caramel ice cream, but that doesn't mean it's good for me. All I'm sayin' is that God may provide you an opportunity to set the record straight, Finn. When He does, don't waste it."*

I had no idea what she meant at the time, but I do now. Jenny must have heard the rumors through the Lake George grapevine but was kind enough to keep them from me. I'm surprised that no one else in town has mentioned anything in the three months that I've been back.

I go upstairs to take a shower and see the walkie-talkie on my nightstand. I switch to the private frequency for the Chief and squawk, "Zimmerman, this is Hollister. Over."

It takes a few seconds, but the Chief responds. "This is Zimmerman. I read you loud and clear. How are you all holding up."

"We're good. I'll be bringing Bailey and the girls home tomorrow morning. Can you pass on the message to the McNamaras?"

"Sure. Sure. That should give you plenty of time to return before the next storm hits. Christmas is supposed to be white-out conditions, and the storm is supposed to gift us with two to three more feet of snow."

I grunt. "Thanks for the heads-up. I'm just checking in and have a question."

"Fire away," he says, laughing at his "firefighter" joke.

"How long have you known that Daniel and Bailey were getting a divorce?" I ask bluntly.

Zimmerman hems and haws. "Since before you moved back here."

I palm my face in frustration. "Why didn't you or anyone else say anything? Even Bryce didn't mention it, and he's friends with Daniel."

"Do you really want to know?"

I nod, although he can't see me. "Please."

Zimmerman clears his throat. "The ink wasn't dry on the divorce until a few weeks ago, Finn. No one wanted to get your hopes up in case they reconciled. I should have warned you that Bailey was returning home once I found out and at least prepared you for the encounter. If it's any consolation, we're all rooting for you now."

I press the talk key with a smile. With nearly the whole town in support of Bailey and I getting together, maybe that second chance Micah is praying for is closer than it appears. "Rah-Rah."

# Chapter Seventeen

## Bailey

Is it wrong that I'm a bit excited that I have another few hours to spend with Finn? It should be since I told him that friendship is the only thing on the menu. Then again, he's been as sweet as the homemade hot chocolate I'm whisking, and he is a rather tempting treat.

Micah comes into the kitchen after a fresh shower and peaks over my shoulder. "Whatcha' makin'?" he asks.

"Sea salt hot chocolate. I thought you might want something to warm your insides after spending all day shoveling snow. Dinner will be ready soon." I ladle some of the creamy liquid into a mug for him, which is the equivalent of Pavlov ringing his bell. All the other kids come over once they hear the first drop hit the bottom of the cup.

Micah goes to the pantry, grabs a bag of miniature marshmallows, putting a small handful into his cup. He pours some into each of their mugs so that there is a layer of ooey gooey goodness on top.

I turn the heat down to low and continue whisking so that the milk doesn't burn. "If you ever want a job, Micah, I'm hiring help once I get my bakery up and running."

"I might take you up on that offer, and I'm sure Finn will approve as long as I get to bring home the day-old pastries," he teases. "And don't forget, as a junior firefighter, I can help you put out the flames when you inevitably burn the muffins because you're staring at a hot firefighter."

A blush creeps across my cheeks. Finn was always pretty to look at, but he's like a fine wine that has gotten better with age. Instead of being simply fit and lean as he was in his youth, now his body is sculpted and muscular. Gone are the boyish features, replaced with a chiseled jawline and rugged look. "I wasn't staring. I was distracted by the mess on the floor."

Ella snorts. "You were distracted by the shirtless man cleaning up the mess. Don't pretend that you weren't."

I ignore Ella and focus on Micah. "If everything goes according to plan, my shop should be open by mid to late spring. Ella will be working there on the weekends."

"Can I work at your shop, too?" Ava asks. "I can be your taste tester!"

I tickle my daughter. "Of course you can. I can pay you in cupcakes!"

Finn finally returns and looks fantastic in a pair of dark-washed jeans and a cream-colored, cable-knit sweater over a burgundy T-shirt. "Sorry that it took me so long. I spoke with Chief Zimmerman, and he says the next storm isn't supposed to hit us until Christmas Day. That should give us plenty of time to get you to your parents' house."

I fix him a mug of cocoa and one for myself before shutting off the burner. "What about the four of you? Are you spending Christmas with your parents, or are you spending it up here?" I ask as I inhale the chocolatey aroma before taking a sip.

He leans against the counter and glances over at the kids. "That was the plan, but with the roads being blocked and the state in lockdown, I doubt they'll make it home in time."

Isaac walks in and rinses out his cup before placing it in the dishwasher. "Grandma and Grandpa went on a cruise to Aruba."

Finn smiles and hands Isaac a paper towel to wipe off his chocolate mustache. "Yes, they did. My dad retired last year from the investment firm, and they have been doing some traveling; mostly to California to help me with the boys. Their flight was supposed to get in tonight, but with the flights being canceled, they're probably enjoying the extra time in Miami."

"Have you tried to call them?" I ask, walking over to the landline and picking up the phone. There still isn't a dial tone. "Never mind."

Finn smirks. "Most people don't have landlines anymore, so fixing it isn't high on the priority list when other things need to be taken care of. Once we get into town, I'll give my parents a call using my cell phone."

I feel bad that Finn and the boys will be spending their first Christmas at Lake George all alone and say as much. "You shouldn't be alone on Christmas."

Finn sips his cocoa. "I have the boys with me, Bailey. I'm not alone. We're together, and that's what matters. As far as my parents are concerned, we'll celebrate together when they get back. I've had to work on Christmas before, and so did Josiah. The boys understand that it's important to celebrate the birth of Jesus, but the day itself doesn't matter."

"Does that mean you'll be coming to the Christmas Eve service if it hasn't been canceled? Pops and Nana do a full spread before we go, and there's plenty of food. You can always join us. Isn't that what friends do?"

One side of Finn's mouth lifts, and the corners of his eyes crinkle. "You know the town is going to gossip if we have dinner with your family. 'Friends' is not what they are going to assume when they see us together."

I take another sip and eye Finn. "They can talk all they want, but it doesn't make it true. It's just two families sharing a meal together. Besides, rumors only seem to travel within a select few. I never heard a peep about what was going on with your sister, and I talk to my mom every week. Even if she knew not to talk about *you* while I was married to Daniel, she didn't tell me anything at all."

Finn shrugs. "My parents mostly came out to visit us in California, and the few times we came home for the holidays, Jenny was doing okay. She specifically asked my parents not to say anything to the town folk because she didn't want the looks of pity that would be thrown her way."

"I miss her," I say. "Because she was away at school, I wasn't as close to her as I was to you. But we had some great talks when she would come home from college."

"She adored you." Finn glances down at his feet. "She never believed what Daniel said. She had more faith in you than I did. I'm so sorry."

I set my mug in the sink now that the drink has gotten cold. I walk over toward the oven and check on the casserole. "What's done is done, Finn, and I need you to stop apologizing. We were both young, and we both made mistakes. I could have fought harder for you or flown to California to confront you, yet I didn't. But we have a clean slate now, right?"

Finn bobs his head. "Right. Can I ask you something?"

"Sure."

"I know you were mad at me and hurt by what I had done, but why did you cut ties with Jenny? She wrote you a letter once, and you wrote back asking her never to write to you again. She loved you like a sister."

I scrunch my nose, confused by what Finn is saying. "What are you talking about? Jenny never wrote to me, and I most certainly didn't write to her telling her to stop all communication. Do you know what her letter said?"

Finn shakes his head. "No. I didn't even know she had sent a letter until she received yours and was really upset. She threw it in the fire and said, 'At least I tried.'"

I purse my lips in dismay. "I promise you, Finn. I never received a letter from your sister. If I had, I would have responded in kind—not coldly or harshly. I've always had too much respect for Jenny to do that."

Ella walks into the room with Micah right behind her. They're carrying the five remaining mugs, which are all empty. Micah rinses the cups and says with a great deal of hesitation, "Maybe it was your hubby?"

Ella begins to snap at Micah for insinuating her father could do such a thing and then thinks better of it. Her shoulders slump. "Micah might be right. Do you remember me saying that I learned of Finn's existence because I overheard Dad talking to his friend Bryce? Dad wanted Bryce to keep you away from Finn. Maybe he intercepted Jenny's letter and wrote back so that Finn wouldn't learn the truth and come back for you."

My heart breaks at the thought. After Daniel and I moved away from Lake George shortly after we were married, the phone calls from the few friends I had stopped abruptly. Until this very moment, I thought it was an "out of sight, out of mind" situation and that we all were busy moving on with our lives. When they didn't answer or return my calls, I eventually gave up and shrugged it off. Now, I have to wonder if it wasn't for entirely different reasons.

"I don't know how your father expected Bryce to keep Finn and me separated. The town only has 3,500 people living in it year-round," I tell her.

Micah bursts out in laughter, then points at Finn. "Bryce has been trying to set up Finn with the single ladies in town. He even convinced Finn to participate in the New Year's Eve Bachelor auction! Bryce's sister, Amanda, is salivating over the chance to ring in the New Year with a kiss from Finn."

Finn scowls at Micah. "You're not helping. Don't you have a video game to play or a brother to taunt?"

Micah smirks. "Not at the moment."

"It's all right, Finn. We're friends, and you can date whomever you please," I say, trying my best not to choke on my words. The timer on the oven starts beeping, giving me the perfect excuse to turn my back toward Finn.

I don't look at him as I pull the bubbling casserole from the oven, but I can feel his eyes boring into me. "Bailey, the auction is for a good cause, and if I had known you were going to be here, I wouldn't have committed to it."

I face the two teens. "Please go and fetch your siblings. Make sure they wash their hands thoroughly. We don't need sticky fingers on the table." They take the hint and give Finn and me a moment of privacy even though we can see the kids sitting in the living room, situated around the coffee table.

Finn steps close so that his body is mere inches from mine. He lowers his voice so that only I can hear. "All you have to do is say the word, and I won't do the auction."

I place my hand over his heart and look up at him with resignation. "Finn, you made a promise. Don't let me stop you from keeping it."

## Chapter Eighteen

### Finn

THE SMELL OF BACON frying coaxes me from my slumber, as do the sounds of children laughing and Christmas music blaring from the stereo in the living room. I groan when I see it's only a quarter past seven and much too early to be awake, but I get up anyway.

I didn't fall asleep until the wee hours of the morning; Bailey's look of disappointment consuming most of my thoughts. Was she disappointed that I was willing to break a promise or that I was being auctioned off in the first place? I pray it was the latter because if it was, then I have a shred of hope that she might want more than to be friends and that we might have a future together. I can work with that.

I brush my teeth and then slip on my robe, ready to greet the day ahead. As I walk down the hall, I start humming along with Jenny's favorite Christmas CD by Home Free playing on the stereo. They're an acapella group with perfect harmony, which is why I don't sing along with them. I'd only ruin the vibe with my howling.

"Good morning!" I shout, startling everyone. Ava has her hand in the cookie jar—literally—and quickly snatches it back when she knows she's been caught. I reach inside, grabbing one of the shortbread cookies to split it with her. I bend down and half-whisper, "Cookies make the best breakfast appetizers."

Ella is directing Jonah, who is standing on a stool and cracking eggs into a bowl. She points at Ava, "Don't let that sweet face fool you. She's had three 'appetizers' already. I doubt Mom is going to be very happy about that."

I scan the room and don't see Bailey anywhere. "Speaking of your mom, where is she?"

Mia answers as she puts premade biscuits onto a baking sheet. "Sleeping. Ella said the smell of bacon would wake her up if the coffee didn't."

I reach for one of the pieces of bacon that Micah has sitting on a paper towel to absorb some of the excess grease. "It woke me up, and I think it smells delicious. Did you all plan on getting up early just to make breakfast?"

Isaac grins while he stirs a pitcher of orange juice concentrate. "We wanted to cook for you and Bailey. You always take care of us, and this morning, we wanted to take care of you! Do you like it?"

I wrap an arm around Isaac's shoulders and squeeze. "I love it! I might have you guys cook every morning from here on out."

Micah laughs. "Don't push it! If Ella and Mia hadn't shown us what to do, we'd be eating cereal for breakfast this morning."

Bailey shuffles in, still half asleep, and makes a beeline for the coffee pot. She yawns as she reaches for a mug and begins pouring. It's not until she takes her first sip that she notices it's the kids who are cooking and not me. Bailey's mouth drops open, and her eyes widen in shock. "Wow! What's all this?"

Jonah stops what he's doing, jumps off his stool and runs to give Bailey a hug. Mia, Isaac, and Ava join him. "It's our Christmas present to you! Our mom used to say that 'acts of service are the best presents in the world because they never break or get shoved in the back of a closet!'"

Bailey's eyes become misty, and she smiles at each and every one of them. "This is the best present I could have gotten. Thank you!" She walks over to Micah and Ella, who are both continuing to cook. She hugs them both. "This is so wonderful!"

Ella winks, "This isn't even the best part."

It's not until Ella and Micah plate our food and then take it into the dining room that I understand what she means. The table is set for two, with a large candle burning inside a glass jar and wine glasses from my cupboard. The plates are filled with fluffy scrambled eggs, bacon, and hot biscuits with a whipped honey butter glaze.

Isaac follows us in with the pitcher of orange juice made from concentrate and pours a glass for us both, spilling a few droplets on the table as he does. He uses the hem of his shirt to wipe it up. "See, Finn! I even cleaned up for you!"

Bailey and I are both giggling when Mia, Jonah, and Ava come in carrying the small portable CD player from the living room. Mia plugs it in while Jonah puts in a CD, most likely from Jenny's Christmas collection. They let Ava contribute by pressing the play button, who gives us two thumbs up and then runs out of the room.

Micah bows and sets a small bell on the table. Using what I presume to be a British accent, he says, "If you need anything, just ring the bell, and one of us will take care of you. Enjoy. Please ring the bell twice when you are finished."

The song "What Child Is This?" plays softly in the background, and Bailey closes her eyes. "This is one of my favorite Christmas songs. Is the 'The Little Drummer Boy' still your favorite?"

"It is. Why don't we pray before the food gets cold? I'd hate for all their hard work to go to waste." I reach for Bailey's hand and can't help but appreciate how her delicate fingers fit into mine as if God made her just for me. When I'd embrace her, her head would fit perfectly underneath my chin, and my arms would fully encompass her small frame.

I clear my throat and my thoughts. "Dear Heavenly Father, we thank You for six amazing children who understand what the Christmas spirit is all about. It's about recognizing the greatest gift of all—Your Son, whom You sent as a sacrifice on our behalf. We thank You for this food, but more importantly, for the hands that prepared it. In your name, Amen."

Bailey echoes the Amen and then picks up her fork to take a bite of eggs. She puts a hand to her mouth and gasps.

"What? Is it that bad?" I ask.

"No! It's that good! Finn, you have to try these! It's the perfect balance of cream, pepper, and salt. They even added some Italian seasoning."

I take a bite and relish the flavor. Putting on airs, I use a hoity-toity accent, which doesn't sound any better than the not-so-British accent Micah had used, "Dare, I say it? These are the best eggs I've ever tasted! I think there's a secret ingredient hidden inside!"

There are a few giggles on the other side of the French doors that separate the dining room from the rest of the house. Ava shouts, "It's because they were made with love!"

"Yes! That's it!" Bailey exclaims. "I thought I tasted a hint of love mixed in."

Eventually, the children leave us alone, and I expect the conversation to be stilted. It isn't. Bailey and I talk for nearly an hour about nothing and everything all at once.

Bailey rubs her tummy as if a mother is caressing her unborn child. "That meal was so good that now I have a food baby."

I set down my fork and then wipe my mouth to hide my snort. "I'm sorry; what? What is a food baby?"

Bailey rubs her belly one more time. "It's when you are so full your stomach sticks out, and it looks like you're five months pregnant."

I rub my belly just as she had. "Then I must be having twins."

She giggles, and then her smile fades and becomes sweeter. "Our kids did an amazing job, and I get the feeling that they want us to be more than friends."

"You do realize they aren't actually my kids, right? They mean well and think that you'll make me happy."

Bailey reaches over and takes my hand. "Micah, Isaac, and Jonah may not be yours by birth, but make no mistake about it, Finn, they are *your* kids. You are now the father figure in their life, and until you get married, you have the honorary title of 'mother figure' as well. Although you're their uncle, one day you'll start referring to them as yours. Just wait and see."

"And what's your take on the 'making me happy' part?" I ask.

She sighs. "I spent years wondering what I would say to you when I came face-to-face with you again, Finn. Never, in a million years, did I think that we could get along after all the hurt feelings and pent-up resentment. I thought I would hate you and that you would hate me, even though I had no idea what I had done."

She raises a hand to stop me from apologizing. "Please don't say 'I'm sorry.' I know you are. But, Finn, you have treated me with nothing but respect and kindness even though you may have thought you had every right to do differently. It shows that you are still the sweet, kind-hearted man that I had fallen in love with so many years ago. Until a few days ago, you believed the worst of me and still took us in without a thought or care as to how it may impact you and your family. You were generous and thoughtful, as were Micah, Isaac, and Jonah."

I squeeze her hand and go out on a limb, asking, "Is there a chance for us in the future?"

"Maybe," she says, brutally honest. "'Future' being the operative word. The fact of the matter is that you *did* believe the worst of me. I want God, love, and trust to be the pinnacle of a relationship. It's going to take time to rebuild the trust, Finn. A part of me will always love you because you were my first true love. That doesn't ever go away. It only changes over time."

"Maybe" is better than a flat-out "No," so I simply dip my chin to acknowledge her words and ring the bell twice.

All six kids rush in and start clearing the table. Ella and Micah stay behind, standing with their hands behind their backs. Bailey looks at them with a raised eyebrow. "Are you waiting for a tip?" she asks jokingly.

Ella points up toward the ceiling, where a plant is haphazardly taped to it. "You are under the mistletoe. You can't leave until you kiss. That's the tradition."

I stare at the dead plant. "That's not mistletoe."

Micah clears his throat. "Actually, it is. Ella and I found it in my mom's scrapbook. That is the same mistletoe Grandpa and Grammy Hollister kissed under at an office Christmas party back in 1972. It was in that moment that they knew they were meant for one another."

"But it's dead!" Bailey says.

Ella grins. "The plant may be dead..."

"But my grandparents' love is still alive," Micah finishes.

Bailey clutches her heart in mock horror. "Oh, no! Finn, they're already finishing each other's sentences. Should we be worried?"

Micah glances at Ella and then shakes his head as if he's dismissing an unwanted thought. "We rehearsed it, so don't go getting any ideas!"

Ella sighs. "Just kiss and get it over with already!"

Bailey leans in and kisses the corner of my lip far too quickly for my liking and because we have an audience. "Done!"

I growl. "Not even close! You totally missed!"

I wrap my hand around Bailey's waist and bring her close to my body. She gasps at the unexpected move, and I use the opportunity to mold my mouth to hers. My other hand slides around the back of her head and grasps the hair at the nape of her neck, tilting her head slightly. My tongue darts out to gently probe, even though my lips are firmly pressed against hers. When I feel the tip of her tongue tease mine, I deepen this kiss, pulling her body flush against mine so that no one would be able to tell where I end and she begins.

Bailey's arms wrap around my neck, and the contented feeling of coming home permeates my body. But we do have an audience, so I dial it back and slow the kiss down, nipping at her lower lip the way she's always loved. The woman I've been madly in love with since I was 15 has a look of pure bliss on her face, and her eyes are closed as if she's been dreaming and doesn't want to wake up. I never want to see that expression on her face for anyone *other* than me. I nip her lower lip one more time and then step back. I say the only thing I can think of in my Bailey-induced-stupor.

"And that's how 'friends' kiss under the mistletoe."

# Chapter Nineteen

## Bailey

*"And that's how 'friends' kiss under the mistletoe."*

Yeah, I've never kissed anyone under the mistletoe before, let alone like the way Finn just rocked my world. I never got to kiss Daniel under the mistletoe because he didn't believe that public displays of affection were appropriate. Finn had no problem telling me without words exactly where he stands and what he wants. I'll admit that it was a kiss that has me rethinking *where* I stand.

Before Finn walks out of the room, he directs Micah to 'gear up, so we can move out.'"

"What about our letters to God?" Micah pleads. "I know we have to take the Johnsons into town, but half an hour of reading our letters won't make a difference."

I want to once again correct Micah that it's McNamara, but after that kiss from Finn, I'm too busy daydreaming about a different last name being attached to me to care. "I think we still have time. It takes, like, two seconds to shove our clothes into our backpacks, Finn. It's not like I brought 15 pairs of shoes to match every outfit or any of my hair and makeup accessories."

Finn smirks. "I kind of like the cartoon reindeer pajama look, especially with the winter boots. As far as makeup and beauty thingamajiggers are concerned, you don't need any of those things to look gorgeous, Bailey."

Finn has always said the sweetest things, but I can't let that affect me. I'm already on the fence about *more* with Finn. "Then you're okay with us doing the whole 'letter' thing before we go?"

"Yeah. We have plenty of time. I just know that your parents, Barb and Henry, are excited to see you," he says.

"My parents will understand, and it's not like they have a time frame in which to expect us. I'm kind of excited to hear what the kids want for Christmas."

Micah gestures for us to follow him. Mia, Ava, Isaac, and Jonah are sitting snugly on the couch. Ella puts a hand on my arm and holds me back. "That was some kiss, Mom. I didn't know you had it in you."

I did. As I reflect on the kiss last night in the basement, I murmur. "I'm sorry if it bothered you to witness the display."

Ella grimaces. "I'm just glad to see someone can make you smile, Mom. It's been a long time since Dad was able to do it. I know that sounds harsh, but I can't recall a time he ever kissed you like that."

I can't bring myself to admit that Daniel had never kissed me like that, not even when we were in private. "Your dad was busy with the restaurant. We just forgot to make time for romance, Ella. My advice to you is that when you get married, continue to date."

"Continue to date?" Ella asks, confused.

"Yep! There's excitement in dating. It feels fresh and new. Even when it isn't, you get to leave the kids at home with a sitter or sneak in a private lunch somewhere other than work. Your dad and I never really did any of that. We just...were. I should have put in more effort to make it work."

At this, Ella scoffs. As the oldest, she understands that I did everything I could and some of the extremes I went through to get Daniel's attention. "And you think dating was the answer?"

"It's about making time for one another, Ella. That's what I'm trying to tell you. Daniel and I stopped doing that. We focused on you girls and the restaurant and forgot about each other."

Ella purses her lips. "It's a two-way street, Mom. I love Dad despite his mistakes, but that doesn't mean I have to condone his actions. You have a man waiting for you in the other room who would give you the world if you let him."

I give my daughter a side hug. "I know, Baby Girl, but I'm scared. I'm scared Finn will run away at the first sign of trouble. I'm scared of him breaking my heart all over again."

"Mom, it's time to open the letters!" Ava shouts, running over to me and dragging me behind her. "I asked God for the bestest thing ever!"

The four youngest take up the oversized couch, and Micah takes the single seat. Ella stands by the tree, ready to go all Vanna White on us. The only spots left for Finn and me are on the loveseat. Once I sit down, I rub my hands back and forth over my thighs. "Okay, Micah. How does this work?"

Jonah raises his hand. "I know! The envelopes get passed out, and we each read one, starting from youngest to oldest. We won't know whose letter we get until we open them!"

Ella collects the envelopes from the tree and passes them out. Ava is the first to open hers and scowls. "I think this one is from Jonah. I can't read the writing." She hands me the letter and sits on my lap while I read it aloud.

*"Dear God,*

*If I could have one thing, it would be my mom and dad. I know you can raise people from the dead, but I also know that you are taking good care of them in Heaven. They like to make funny jokes, so you probably want to keep them with you. But if I can't have them, then maybe you can give us Bailey, Ava, Mia, and Ella. I love them.*

*Love,*
*Jonah"*


Ava looks up at me with a smug expression. "I told you it was from Jonah! His writing is as good as his artwork!"

Jonah's lips turn down. "My mom said my writing is as good as a doctor's!"

I gesture to the twins. "Which one of you is the youngest?" I ask, getting them back on track. "Jonah, that was a very sweet letter. Is it your turn?"

Isaac rips open his envelope. "Nope. Jonah was born eight minutes before me. It's my turn.

*"Dear Jesus,*

*Life doesn't always turn out as we expected, but you have greater plans in store for us. You tell us "No" when we're not ready, "Yes" when we are. Sometimes you say, "Not right now." I've learned to accept your answers because you give them to us in love. You give them to us to protect us. You give them to us because you know better than we do. But that isn't going to stop me from asking for one more thing. Heavenly Father, I ask that you protect Bailey and her family. Help them find healing and happiness.*

*Love,*
*Finn"*

Once again, Finn only wants to see others free from pain. He's a hero through and through. "That was...I have no words, Finn." He smiles at me.

"My turn!" Jonah declares. He opens the letter in his hand and starts reading.

*"Dear God,*

*I don't have much to ask, but I have so much to be thankful for. I thank You for my Mom and my sisters. I thank You for my Dad. I thank you for letting us get stuck in a storm so that I could make new friends. I thank You for bringing a smile to my mom's face. It's been so long since I've seen it. Mom says I'm too young to know what's going on, but I'm not. I see it. I also see how Finn makes her face light up just by walking into the room. I know what I should be praying for, but all I want is for my mom to be happy. Will you make that happen?*

*Your friend,*
*Mia"*

That's a pretty deep letter for a ten-year-old, but then again, Mia is wiser than her years. I can't tell from her letter if she's asking for a second chance between Finn and me or between her father and me. In the end, she's simply asking for God's will to be done. "I love you, Mia. You and your sisters make me very happy."

Mia hugs me back. "I love you, too, Mom."

"It's your turn, Mia!" Ava says.

Mia reverently runs her finger under the seal and pulls out the sheet of paper.

*"Dear God,*
*I want Finn and Bailey to get together.*
*The End,*
*Isaac"*

Well, all right then. "That was short, sweet, and to the point," I tell him.

We continue to read the notes aloud, with both Micah and Ella asking that Finn and I take a leap for love. In my letter, I ask God to keep everyone safe through the snowstorm and to protect the workers who are braving the cold so that people can have electricity and heat to stay warm.

Finn is the last to go, and Ava's letter is the only one left. I pull Ava into my lap as we listen to Finn read the note.

*"Deer Jesus,*
*Can I pleez half a Barbie Jeep for Crismas?*
*Ava"*

Finn shows us the letter, and I laugh. Ava is six and is learning to write out words based on how they sound to her little ears. There is a drawing at the bottom of the page of Christmas trees and a stick figure driving a box with two circles. She also drew snowflakes to decorate the letter.

"This is a masterpiece," Finn tells her.

Ella folds her arms across her chest and narrows her eyes playfully at Ava. "I think you missed the point of the letters. We were supposed to ask for one *intangible* thing from God."

Ava frowns. "Well, I don't know what that word means, and I really want a Barbie Jeep! Maybe there is one waiting for me at Pops' and Nana's house!"

And that's our cue that we need to leave. Finn tells the boys to take quick showers and get ready while the girls and I get dressed and stuff everything in our backpacks. Once we're ready to go, Finn leads us upstairs and shows us where we'll be exiting. The snow drifts are piled high, reaching two feet below the window frame. "Every time I look out the window, I'm blown away by the amount of snow. I can't thank you enough for taking us in. You and the boys saved our lives, and we're forever in your debt."

Finn and Micah strap on their snowshoes, and Micah goes out the window first. He starts walking around the house to get one of the ATVs that's parked under the back deck. We would go out the mudroom door in the basement, but it, too, is blocked by snow since it's on the side of the house.

"How come we don't jump off the back porch?" Mia asks.

Finn crawls through the window, but before he leaves, he answers Mia's question. "There isn't as much snow on the backside of the house, and the distance is too great for you to jump safely. I wouldn't want you to get hurt. You mean too much to us. You all do."

I watch as Finn disappears around the side of the house, and a few minutes later, the two ATVs appear. Since we don't have snowshoes and would fall through the soft flakes, Finn and Micah carry us from the window to the vehicles.

Jonah rides with us, but he opts to sit in the back with Ava so that I can have the front seat. Finn shouts over the roar of the engine. "Are you ready to go home?"

I bob my head but remain silent, with only one thought crossing my mind. *Finn feels like home. He always has.*

# Chapter Twenty

## Finn

We head over the hill toward the lakeside highway, and my eyes widen when I notice that the roads have been cleared. We do a quick pass by Bailey's food truck and see that it's gone. "The road crews must have been working non-stop for the past day and a half," I say, thinking out loud.

"Where's my truck?" Bailey asks, panicking.

I press the button on my walkie-talkie and connect with Zimmerman. "Chief, the roads are clear, and Bailey's food truck is gone. Any idea where it might be?"

Zimmerman gives us the down low. "It's at Mike's garage. A few of the town folk helped dig it out so that Mike could tow it. It's standard policy for abandoned vehicles, but Mike isn't charging for the tow. He says Merry Christmas, by the way!"

Bailey visibly relaxes and snatches the radio from me. "Merry Christmas, Chief! Tell Mike we say 'Hi!' and will see him at the service this evening!"

I snatch the radio out of her hands and give her a stern look. "The radio is for official use only."

"I was officially saying 'Merry Christmas,'" she retorts. I shake my head and chuckle.

It takes us about half an hour to get into town, and we park in front of the McNamara home. It's a beautiful bed and breakfast with eight rooms and a large front porch. As we head up the salted walkway, I ask, "Are you sure that Barb and Henry will be all right with four extra mouths to feed? Six, if you take into consideration how much a teenage boy can eat."

"You've had Christmas Eve dinner with us before, Finn. My mom doesn't know how to cook for less than a dozen people during the holidays. If you guys don't join us, then we'll be eating ham and cornbread pudding for a month!"

Bailey is right, and her mother, Barbara, invites us to stay before we even have a chance to take our coats off. Bailey's parents hug their daughter and granddaughters first, but they welcome us with open arms and with equal affection. When Barb hugs me, she whispers, "Thank you for taking care of my babies, Finn. Once we learned that they were with you, we knew that they were in good hands."

I hug her back. "The pleasure was ours, Barb. It gave Bailey and me the opportunity we needed to clear the air and discover the truth. I don't know if we would have ever had the kind of heart-to-heart we had if we hadn't been stuck together."

Barb releases her hold on me and steps back. "God does work in mysterious ways. What was this truth that you discovered?"

I glance over at Bailey, who is hanging up the coats. "I'll leave that one for Bailey to tell you."

Barb quickly puts me to work in the kitchen before disappearing upstairs, dragging Bailey behind her. I assume it's because she can't wait to get the inside scoop, and I'm right. Ten minutes later, she returns with tears glistening in her eyes. "I guess the silver lining is that you have a second chance with Bailey, although she assures me the two of you are just friends."

"Yep. What Bailey wants, Bailey gets," I say, listening to everyone laugh at something on the television.

"But what do you want, Finn?" Barb asks.

"I want Bailey to be happy. I don't want to rush her into a relationship, and if friends are all we'll ever be, then I can live with that."

She turns off the burners and takes the foil off the ham that's been resting. "That's the thing, Finn. She is happier than I've seen her in a long time, and it's only been an hour. I don't think you'll have to wait long for her to realize what we all see in the time you've been here. Despite Daniel's lies, I do believe he truly loved Bailey, and I know Bailey loved him. A part of her always will, just as a part of her has always loved you. Yet, there was always something missing in their relationship. Maybe it was the spark that keeps the fire going. You know, the one that never really goes out, but with a soft breath, it can reignite a passion and turn into an inferno of everlasting love. You and Bailey have that spark. You always have."

I go over to the sink and begin washing the pots and pans that have slowly piled up. "Barb, how come you never spoke to Bailey about me or warned her that I moved back to Lake George with my nephews?"

"I didn't think it was wise while Bailey and Daniel were married. You and Bailey had both moved on. It was out of respect for their marriage that I kept my mouth shut. As to why I didn't warn her about your return, that's a no-brainer. I was afraid she would choose to make her fresh start somewhere else just to avoid you."

"I guess I was surprised that no one in this town said a word—to her or to me. It almost feels like it's a conspiracy," I tease.

Barb barks out a laugh, then winks. "I will neither confirm nor deny. What I will say is that everyone is rooting for the two of you."

·♥·♥·♥·♥·♥·

Dinner was amazing, and so was the Christmas Eve church service. The recounting of Christ's birth never gets old and brings me to tears every time I hear it. To know that our Father sent His Son in human form to be a sacrifice to atone for our sins is the greatest gift we could receive.

Bailey nudges me as we amble from the church to the house, which is two blocks away. "Because of the weather, there is room at the inn," she jokes. "You and the boys should stay in the guest rooms and then spend Christmas morning with us. It's dark outside, and it isn't safe to travel at night."

I open my mouth, but she keeps on rambling. "You can't use the excuse of another storm coming because it's moving south now and isn't going to hit us. Plus, your parents texted and said they'd be landing in Albany in the morning and should be home by noon. It would be a waste of gas for you to ride the ATVs back to your place only to have to come right back."

Reaching out for Bailey's hand to stop her verbal spewing, I spin her around to face me. In doing so, she loses her footing on the ice, with me barely catching her before her butt hits the ground. She scrambles to get her feet under her, but she can't find purchase on the slick sidewalk. I drag Bailey over to her neighbor's yard, both of us falling in the snow.

Yanking my glove off with my teeth, I caress her rosy cheeks with my fingers. "Why do you want us to spend Christmas with you, Bailey? Is it because you feel pity for us?"

She glances at the six kids having a snowball fight in the front yard having a blast, then back at me. "Pity is the last thing I feel for you, Finn."

I wrap my hand around her waist, and her hands grip my biceps. I smirk and flex underneath to tempt and tantalize her. "What *do* you feel for me, Bailey Bug?"

Before she can answer, Ava screams with excitement and draws our attention. "Daddy! You came to see us!"

Bailey removes her hands quickly as if she's been burned and gets up to march over in her daughter's direction to find out what's going on. I catch up to her and stop in my tracks when I watch Daniel pick Ava up and swing her around. He gives each of his daughters a hug and then embraces Bailey, who does not hug him back. "What are you doing here, Daniel?" she asks curtly. "Aren't you supposed to be getting married tomorrow?"

Daniel notices that he has an audience. "May we speak in private?" he asks. Without waiting for an answer, he turns around and walks 20 yards away.

Bailey turns to the girls, "Go ahead and go inside. I'll just be a few minutes." Barb and Henry usher the girls into the house, leaving the boys and me outside feeling awkward. She gently places her hand on my arm. "My offer still stands. You're welcome to stay and spend Christmas with us. I just need a minute to figure things out and find out why he's here."

I gently press my lips against hers and leave it up to Bailey to determine if it's a kiss goodbye. "I'll take the boys to my parents' house since I have a key. We'll spend Christmas there. The girls should spend the holiday with their father, not someone they just met four days ago. You know where to find me when you get things 'figured out.'"

Bailey lowers her gaze and mumbles, "So, you're just going to walk away?"

I lift her chin with my gloved hand. "I'm not walking away from you. Not this time. I'm going to respect and trust you by giving you the space to make your decision without any pressure or expectations. You know how I feel about you and what I want. The next move is yours. Until then, Merry Christmas."

I wave the boys over, and we climb into the ATVs and drive the six blocks to the other end of town where my parents live.

Micah gets out of the ATV and slams the door. "Are you really just going to let her go, Finn? Aren't you going to fight for her?"

"Bailey doesn't need me to fight her battles, Micah, and our staying would only make the situation awkward and uncomfortable for everyone. She needs someone who is patient and understanding and who can trust and support her. I'm that guy, but Bailey has to come to that realization on her own."

# Chapter Twenty-One

## Bailey

My heart sinks as I watch Finn and the boys drive away, and the cold I hadn't felt previously now permeates my body. I pull my hat a little further down on my head and spin on my heel, which is a bad idea because I lose my balance on the slick asphalt and windmill my arms as I try to stay upright. I epically fail and end up on my butt.

Daniel walks over to me and doesn't even bother to offer me a hand to help me up, expecting me to do it myself. I eventually get to my feet and stare up at my ex. "You got your wish, and we're alone. Will you tell me why you're here?"

"I came to spend time with the girls," he says.

"A little warning would have been nice." I brush the snow from my body and shake out my hair.

"I tried calling you for three days! You didn't answer, Bailey!"

I frown. "I wasn't in a place with cell reception, Daniel. Tell me, why are you *really* here? Aren't you supposed to be getting married to Delaney tomorrow?"

"Delaney and I called off the wedding shortly after you left. Afterward, I was sitting in our home, and it was so quiet. I started questioning my life choices and the man that I had become. I didn't like him, Bailey. The sound of laughter was missing, and I was lonely. I didn't realize how hard it would be once you and the girls were gone. And..."

"And what? Did Bryce tell you that we were at Finn's place and that you had to come and stop me from making a terrible mistake? Are you here to lie to me yet again?"

Daniel's cheeks redden, but not out of anger or from the cold, but from embarrassment. "He told you."

I poke my fingers in his chest, and my blood begins to boil. "Of course he did! Finn left me because you lied to him, Daniel! You told him that I had been cheating on him with you behind his back! You manipulated the situation to your advantage. Did you honestly think that wouldn't come out once I returned home? Is that why you wanted Bryce to keep Finn and me apart? So that I wouldn't learn the truth?"

Daniel stutters over his words. "I, uh. Um."

"You are unbelievable! Go home to Delaney and work it out. Go get your happily ever after." I stomp a few feet away, then spin back around. "You know what? Here's what I don't understand, Daniel. Finn was your best friend as much as I was. Why would you do that to him or to me?"

"Because I had been in love with you since the ninth grade, Bailey! Then Finn came along with his good looks, talent, and smarts, and suddenly, my chance with you evaporated. I was biding my time thinking that he would mess up or that the two of you would break up, but then you guys started talking about marriage," he says, finally being the most honest with me he's ever been.

"So, you lied to Finn to get him out of the picture, and then you lied to me. You manipulated me. And for what? So that you could sell *our* restaurant by forging my signature, and then divorce me when I wasn't good enough for you anymore?"

Daniel holds his hands out, pleading. "You were more than good enough for me! It was me that was never good enough for you! I messed up big time, Bailey! From the beginning, our relationship was built on lies—lies that I told. All I wanted was for you to be mine, but the guilt at what I had done was eating away at me! I couldn't stand to look at myself in the mirror anymore, but instead of coming to you with the truth, I sought solace elsewhere. For that, I am truly sorry. You never deserved what I did. I didn't know it then because I was young and selfish, but Finn was the better man. He always has been."

"Are you here to ask for a second chance?" I ask bluntly.

He holds up his hands in surrender and shakes his head. "I'm here to see the girls and to ask for your forgiveness. I never should have lied. I never should have cheated. And I never should have done those despicable things. But the one thing that is true and always will be is that I love our girls with every ounce of my being. I realized that I haven't told them that enough, and the only way to make that right is to be there for them moving forward."

I eye him skeptically. I know when Daniel is hiding something. "Is that all?"

Daniel steps back and runs a hand through his hair. "I do want to see our girls, Bailey. That is if you'll let me. I'd like to spend Christmas with them while I'm here and tell them I love them."

My anger dissipates. "I'll never stop you from spending time with our girls, Daniel. They love you no matter what. Come over tomorrow morning at eight, and I'll ensure they're up. Where are you staying, and for how long?"

He grimaces. "I was hoping to stay here since my parents' home is buried in snow, but I'll be leaving tomorrow to arrange my belongings to be moved to their final destination."

"And where might that be?" I ask.

He hooks a thumb over his shoulder in the direction of his childhood home about five doors down from ours. "Here, in Lake George. My father is going to have me take over his accounting practice so that he and my mom can stay in South Carolina full-time, and they'll let me live in their house."

Oh, you have got to be kidding me! Daniel plans on coming home for a fresh start! Doesn't he know that I have the monopoly on that sort of thing?

I point toward the front door. "I can't deal with this right now. Please go inside and spend time with our daughters since that's why you're here. I need time to think, and I'll make up a bed for you when I get back."

His eyebrows raise in surprise. "Aren't you coming in?"

"Not right now. I'm going to go for a much-needed walk." I zip up my coat so that it covers my mouth and put my hands in my jacket pockets. Having fallen several times already, I think better of it and let my arms hang loose. I'll need them for stabilization purposes—of that, I have no doubt.

I wait for Daniel to go inside before heading in Finn's direction. It takes me nearly half an hour to go the six blocks, but I use the time to think about Finn and his kind heart. Daniel didn't even bother to help me up, yet Finn never wanted to leave my side. Despite Finn's belief I had wronged him, he didn't hesitate to rescue us and make us feel like we belonged.

The only reason Finn left me tonight was to give me the space he thought I needed. At the time, I wanted him to stay with me while I spoke with Daniel because I thought I might need him for support. But Finn believed I had the strength to handle the situation and trusted me to do so. If I had begged him to stay, I know he would have.

I had no idea that coming home would provide me with closure from past hurts and a pathway to forgiveness. I had no idea that a fresh start might include a second chance to get things right. I thought that if I were to ever cross paths with Finn, we were certainly going to be enemies. Okay, "enemies" isn't the right word because other than the one mistake that ultimately ended us, we almost never argued. But I definitely didn't consider the notion of us becoming friends again a possibility. Ella probably would have called us "frenemies."

The more I think about Finn and how God placed him in our path at precisely the right time and place when we needed help, the clearer my decision becomes. Finn and I were brought together for a reason, and I would be a fool to question His plan for me—for us.

I desperately want to cross the street and knock on the door to share my feelings and declare my intentions, but something in my gut stops me. Maybe it's the fact all the lights are out or that Daniel is staying in our home and spending Christmas with our girls. Regardless of the reason, I can't ignore the nagging feeling that I need to wait.

After wandering around the town and doing some soul-searching, I finally come full circle and arrive at my childhood home. My mom is waiting up for me. "Where is everyone?" I ask as I hang up my coat and remove my boots.

She pats the seat next to her, gesturing for me to sit. "You were gone for three hours, Bailey. Everyone is asleep, so it's just you and me. I stayed up because I thought you might want to talk."

I told her the reason behind Daniel's arrival and that he would be leaving tomorrow so that he could move here. She nods and says, "I wondered if he would ever see the light and get his priorities straight, but he took you up on your advice and doted on the girls while you were gone. It's an answered prayer. However, I don't think he took it well when the girls couldn't stop talking about Finn and his nephews."

Ella tiptoes down the stairs, but the creak of the last step gives her away. She comes over and snuggles herself in between my mom and me. She grins. "In all fairness, Dad did ask what it was like being trapped in a cabin. All we did was tell him the truth." Ella leans her head on my shoulder. "Are you going to get back together with Dad? Is that why he's really here?"

I gently stroke her hair. "No, Baby, I'm not. That's not why he's here. He's here for you, Mia, and Ava. He wants to have a relationship with you and is doing the right thing." As much as it might be awkward having Daniel down the street, at least working out visitation isn't going to be an issue.

"How are you okay with this? How can you forgive him so easily?" Ella asks. My mom raises her eyebrow at me, wondering how I'm going to tackle this one.

"It's not easy, Ella, but if I don't, I'll harbor a resentment that will eat away at me. Forgiveness isn't about just saying the words; it's a state of the heart. That means that I have to forgive over and over again until I don't have to remind myself to do it. I loved your father, and a part of me always will. That love just isn't the romantic kind of love anymore."

"Do you still love Finn in the romantic sense?" she asks.

I smirk. "Finn was my first love, Ella. There will always be a special connection between us. Could I love him in that way again? The answer is a resounding 'Yes!'"

"Then you need to show him with a grand gesture, and I know just what you should do." Ella rubs her hands together and lays out her plan. I have to admit, it's a good one.

・♥・♥・♥・♥・♥・

The following day is a frenzy of activity as the girls open their presents and the adults sit around and bask in their joy. Daniel has his bags packed and sitting by the door, but he stays long enough to have breakfast with us and spend more time with our daughters.

"A Barbie Jeep!" Ava shouts after tearing through the paper of her last gift. "God answered my letter! Wahoo! Thank you!"

When Daniel looks confused, Ella explains the Hollister family tradition of writing letters to God. Thankfully, she has enough tact not to tell her dad what *she* asked for.

Daniel clears his throat. "It's time for me to leave. I have a plane to catch, and although the roads are clear, it's still going to be slow going." He embraces each of the girls and says his goodbyes, promising to see them soon. "Bailey, will you walk me to my car?"

I silently answer by bundling up to brace the cold. Once we're at his rental vehicle, he turns to me and says, "I'm sorry for everything I did. You deserve to be happy. I know I'm not the man to do that, and I just want to say that I wish you the best."

I open my mouth to say something snarky, but he puts a finger to my lips. "I know what you're thinking, Bailey, but I promise not to stand in the way of that happiness. I will not interfere in your life, but I do want to be a part of Ella's, Mia's, and Ava's. Maybe at some point in the future, you and I can be friends again."

"I can't stop you from moving home, and the girls are thrilled to have you close, but I won't tolerate you spreading any more lies, Daniel. It's not fair to the girls, Finn, or me. If friendship is something you really want, that is the first step you'll need to take."

"You have my word, Bailey. I know that doesn't mean much to you right now, but I want it to mean something moving forward. I know that our daughters love me unconditionally, but I want them to *like* me, too. I want them to look up to me and talk about me the way they did about Finn last night. I'm jealous, but not because he gets the girl in the end. I'm jealous because he's the kind of man who deserves to."

I tear up. "He is, but you can be that man, too. It's never too late."

Daniel wraps his arms around me and kisses the top of my head. "I'm counting on that. Merry Christmas, Bailey."

"Merry Christmas, Daniel." I kiss his cheek and step out of the embrace just as Finn and the boys drive by in their ATV.

Finn doesn't look my way, but Micah frowns and shakes his head in disappointment. I watch them continue until they pull into the fire station down the road, realizing that I need to do some damage control.

I wave to Daniel and then head back inside. "Ella, I need your help!" I plop down on the sofa beside her and explain what just happened outside. My girls are excited to learn that their dad will be moving to town, but Ella is all business when it comes to helping me rectify the situation.

"I'll text Micah and let him in on our plan and explain that what he saw wasn't what it looked like," she says, typing away on her phone. "It's so good having cell service again."

We wait on pins and needles until Micah finally texts back. Ella shows me the phone and grins. "Micah apologizes for jumping to conclusions, and he wants to know how he can help."

"Text him back and let him know to keep our plan a secret and don't let Finn renege on his promise. I'm counting on Finn to do the right thing."

Micah replies with a thumbs-up emoji.

I smile. "Operation Win Finn" is in full effect.

# Chapter Twenty-Two

## Finn

When I drove by Bailey's home on Christmas morning, I couldn't help but notice that Daniel's rental car was still parked out front. As I got closer, I saw the couple embracing on the sidewalk and Bailey giving Daniel a kiss on the cheek. I had to look away while Micah continued to stare at them in disbelief. His disappointment was evident, but it didn't last long.

Shortly after I pulled into the fire station, Micah's phone pinged with a text, and he disappeared for the next hour while I hung out with the guys working their shift. Isaac and Jonah spent most of that time climbing on the fire trucks.

Right as we were about to leave, Bryce walked up to me and slapped me on the back. "Guess who's moving to Lake George?"

"Other than Bailey and her daughters, I don't have a clue," I told him.

He laughed. "Daniel. He texted me this morning and said he broke it off with his fiancée and is moving back here. It's all but a done deal. He's heading to Myrtle Beach to pack up his stuff, and he'll be back by New Year's Eve."

I barely held back the grimace from all the salt Bryce was rubbing in my wound and shrugged it off. "Thanks for the heads up."

He clasps his hand on my shoulder. "I felt it was my civic duty to keep you in the loop so that you don't get any ideas of trying to come between them. They have three daughters who need their father, Finn. The bright side is my sister is looking forward to her New Year's Eve date with you."

I remove his hand from my shoulder. "I don't think I'm really in the mood to be auctioned off to the highest bidder."

Micah strolled up to us, still texting on his phone. Without looking at me, he said, "You should keep your promise, Finn. What kind of example would you be setting for Isaac, Jonah, and me if you didn't? It's one date for a good cause, and who knows? It could turn into forever if you let it."

And that's how I find myself standing here behind the stage and sweating bullets. Despite my reservations about the auction and learning that the rumors of Daniel's return are true, I find myself decked out in a tux, ready to become someone's date tonight.

Micah, who is also dashing in his dark suit, adjusts my bow tie. "Don't be nervous, Finn. It's a few hours on the arm of a lovely lady and a kiss to ring in the New Year. Remember that all the proceeds go to the Pediatric Burn Unit at the hospital in Albany."

"There's only one woman I have any interest in dating, and she's unavailable. I waited all week for Bailey to come to me and explain what I saw, but she didn't," I tell him.

"I sense a bit of history repeating itself. Have you confronted Bailey and asked her outright what her intentions are?" Micah asks, yanking a little harder on the tie than necessary.

"I promised I would give her space and that the next move is hers. I didn't expect a week of radio silence," I admit.

Micah lets go and shrugs. "A lot happened in a short period of time, and I'm sure it was overwhelming for her.

If I had more than five dollars in my pocket for the concessions, I'd bet you she appreciated the space and time to breathe. You offered her friendship, which she sorely needs. Is that still on the table if she gets back together with Daniel? Be honest because I know you offered it with the intent that it could turn into more."

I don't answer him right away because I also offered that hand of friendship believing that Daniel wouldn't be in the picture full-time. Now that he is, it changes my perspective. I swallow hard, not because I'm nervous, but because Micah re-tied my bow too tight. I pull at the bow tie to loosen it slightly.

I open my mouth to answer when a throat clears from the darkened corner off to our right. A deep voice tells Micah, "That's not really a fair question to ask a man in love. If you were in love with a girl—could you stand by and be her friend while she was in love with someone else. Could you be her friend without letting jealousy grip you and guide your actions? Could you pretend that you weren't head over heels for the girl?"

Micah shakes his head as the man emerges from the shadows. The corners of Daniel's lips turn up when he sees me. He turns to face Micah, "May I have a moment alone with your uncle?"

I give Micah a subtle nod that he should leave. I turn to Daniel. "Are you here to gloat?"

His smile fades. "Quite the contrary. I'm here to apologize."

My face must register my surprise because he chuckles and then continues, "I've always admired and respected you, Finn, although I never told you or showed you because I was jealous of you from the moment you came to town and caught Bailey's eye. I pretended to be your friend so that I could be hers. It wasn't fair to either of you, and for that, I'm sorry."

"You're sorry? You lied to get what you wanted and took away the one person who meant the world to me. I've accepted that I played a part in believing the lies and assuming the worst, but I never thought you would betray me, Daniel. I trusted and loved you like a brother. When you told me that you had been cheating behind my back, you did it with such remorse that I didn't even question it. I questioned Bailey's integrity instead! And the Academy Award goes to Daniel Johnson for Best Actor."

Daniel's shoulders slump, and his chin reaches his chest. "I deserve that. You have every right to hate me."

Some of the vehemence leaves my body as I deflate. "I don't hate you, Daniel. I just wish I understood why."

He clasps his hands behind his back and stares at the ground. "Because I'm not a good man, Finn. At least not compared to you. I want to be. I want my daughters to speak of me the way they spoke of you on Christmas Eve. You've always put other people first, but not me. I've been selfish, and now I've lost the best things to ever happen to me. I'm here to get some of that back."

"You're here for Bailey."

He shakes his head. "If I had tried, she would have shot me down like an F-22 taking down a hot air balloon. Quick, decisive, and with more ammunition than necessary to get the job done. We have a lot of good memories together, but I broke the cardinal rule. She may have forgiven me, but I don't deserve a second chance, nor do I want one. I just want Bailey to get the 'happily ever after' she was supposed to get in the first place."

My heart lifts at his admission. "Then why are you moving back?"

He laughs. "Do you want the truth?" He waits for me to nod. "First and foremost, I'm moving back for my daughters. It's hard to maintain a relationship with them if there are 1,500 miles between us. I'd have to take them away from their friends for summers and holidays, and they wouldn't want that. Even though Bailey and I are over, I'm not willing to give up on my girls."

I can and absolutely respect that. "And the other reason?"

"Free rent and a job," he says jokingly, only I don't think he's kidding. "Look, Finn, I'm not planning on getting in the way if Bailey and you decide to rekindle an old relationship. I had my chance and blew it big time. I just wanted to let you know that I'm sorry for the way I treated you and for my actions. Bailey was never meant to be mine, no matter how much I wanted her to be. I will be in my daughters' lives and Bailey's by default. I'll be at family barbecues and such. You should know that if you pursue a relationship with her, I promise to be on my best behavior—no more lies and or manipulation."

He holds out his hand for me to shake. I eye it warily but slide my palm into his. "Can you do me a favor?"

"Name it. I owe you one for all the pain I caused you. I was young and selfish, Finn, and thinking in the moment. I never thought about the impact in the long term."

I squeeze his hand and pull him close, speaking in low tones. "Can you tell Bryce your plans? He's your biggest advocate, and not a day goes by that I don't beg God and say, 'Hold me back!'"

Daniel laughs. "I can do that. I'll also give you some fair warning. His sister, Amanda, has saved up to get a date with you tonight."

I cringe. "How much?"

"Enough to buy a used car?" he jokes. His smile fades, and his tone becomes serious. "I can't change the past, Finn, but I can promise a better future. I doubt we'll ever be friends, but I'd like to be. At a minimum, I'd like for us to be cordial. The best way I know to do that is to ask for your forgiveness. If you can't grant it, I understand."

I embrace Daniel, and we give each other the three-pat 'bro' hug. "If you are truly remorseful, I forgive you. But it's not my forgiveness that matters in the end. Why don't you come to church next Sunday? I'll save a seat for you."

He smiles. "I might just take you up on that offer. Good luck with the auction. I hope you make a very lucky lady happy tonight."

Bryce walks off the stage and notices that Daniel and I are standing side by side. He looks perplexed by the amicable expressions on our faces and then goes into full "Bryce" mode. "I just raked in $2,300, a record for the department. Beat that Hollister!"

"Tell me, Bryce, how much did your sister save to get a date with me?"

His eyes narrow. "She only has to beat the highest bidder; it doesn't mean she has to spend everything."

I laugh. "She saved that much, huh?" I let the thought hang in the air as the Emcee continues the auction.

And now we introduce our next and final bachelor of the evening," the host of the evening says. "He graced our town with his presence 20 years ago at the ripe old age of 16, then vanished into thin air. In that time, he has been lauded as a hero, saving countless lives and thousands of homes from wildfires on the West Coast. He's a qualified smokejumper with enough muscles to tear down trees with his bare hands. He can leap tall buildings in a single bound, and tonight, he can be your prince who rescues you from the New Year doldrums with a kiss to ring in the New Year! Welcome the Ghost of Christmas Past, Finn Hollister!"

And the crowd goes wild!

I walk out onto the stage and then unbutton my suit jacket, striking a pose and tossing my head back. People laugh as I do a fake model walk, and someone from the crowd yells, "Work it, Hollister! Work it!"

The Emcee starts the bidding. "Do I hear $500?"

"$500!" Bryce's sister, Amanda, shouts.

"$600!" says a voice in the back. I narrow my eyes to see through the bright light, but I can't make out the identity of the second bidder.

"$700!" Amanda says, scowling at the woman.

"$1,000!" the woman says, slowly making her way through the crowd. Bailey comes into sight, dressed to the nines in a deep scarlet dress with a single sleeve on her shoulder. The form-fitting attire hugs her every curve. Her make-up is done flawlessly, and she looks natural and beautiful. I'll admit, she looks stunning, but the thought of her with a messy bun, reindeer pajama pants, and snow boots gets my heart thumping.

$2,000!" Amanda says.

Bailey's mom and dad stand behind her, as do her three girls. "$2,500!" her mom shouts.

Amanda doesn't relent. $3,500! Bailey, you had your chance with Finn. Now it's my turn!" she screeches.

I palm my face as the bidding war continues. When the temperature in the room begins to rise, I get a not-so-bright idea and strip off my jacket. Amanda becomes so flustered she outbids herself and shouts, $4,000!"

Bailey's face falls, the price becoming too rich for her blood. Chief Zimmerman leans over toward Bailey and whispers in her ear. She whispers something back, and he smiles, giving her a gentle squeeze. "$4,500!" he shouts.

The Emcee sputters. "Um, Chief, you can't date your own crew. It's against policy."

Zimmerman laughs. "I'm helping out true love. I don't plan on kissing anyone other than my wife tonight!"

Amanda scowls. "$6,000! First, you got Finn, but then you got Daniel. Why do you get all the good men in this town?!"

One of our other probies yells from the back of the crowd, "I'm available for free Amanda! Go out with me!"

Daniel comes up behind Bailey and joins everyone else who is supporting this bidding war. He smiles at me. He wraps his arms around his daughters, and I feel my jealousy spike until he stands up straighter and says, $10,000!"

The Emcee sputters. "Um. Uh. I know Finn is hot, but is he really *that* hot?"

Daniel laughs. "You can't put a price on true love!" Then he realizes what he's said and amends, "True love between Bailey and Finn! Not Finn and me!"

Amanda realizes that the whole town will rally behind Bailey, but she gives it one last go. $10,500!"

I pull out my phone and check the balance in my savings account as the Emcee says, "10,500 going once!"

"Two seconds!" I shout as my account begins to load.

"Going twice!"

I look at her with mock contempt. "Two seconds!

And...

$10, 672!" I shout. "Amanda, you're a sweet lady, but that woman right there is my future," I say, pointing to Bailey.

The Emcee pulls the mike away from her mouth and whispers, "You can't bid on yourself, Finn."

I take the mike from her hand and say, "If I have my way, it's going to end up being a joint account anyway!"

The crowd whoops and hollers as I hand the microphone back to the Emcee and jump on the floor. The crowd parts like we're in a 1980's John Hughes film. Bailey walks toward me as I walk toward her, and we meet in the middle.

"Sold!" The Emcee shouts as if I have given her any choice.

The spotlight shines down on us, and I block my eyes from the brightness. "Sorry, Finn," the guy says, dimming the light but not taking it off us.

I cup Bailey's cheek. "Please tell me I'm not dreaming and that I really did spend ten grand so that I can kiss you."

"I don't have a penny to my name at the moment, but I would have taken out a second mortgage for a second chance with you, Finn. You're worth it."

I draw Bailey close and lean down to press my lips against hers. Her lips part, inviting me in. I'm not one to decline an invitation and readily accept.

"It's not the New Year yet! Save it for three hours, 47 minutes, and 12 seconds from now. Eleven! Ten," someone yells.

Then another person chides, "The countdown doesn't begin until ten seconds until New Year, Earl!"

The world fades around me as I peck and nip at Bailey's plump lips. "Does this mean you don't want to be friends?" I tease her.

She wraps her arms around me and nuzzles my neck. She whispers in my ear, "I want to be friends, Finn. But I also want so much more."

Ava runs up to us along with the rest of our family and shouts, "Group hug!"

I smile because I wouldn't have it any other way.

# Epilogue

## Bailey -- Six Months Later

"Keep your eyes closed," my husband, Finn, says as he walks behind me with his hands over my eyes. "Otherwise, you'll ruin the surprise!"

We've been married for two months now, and the wedding was a beautiful, chaotic mess. It was supposed to be a small affair at the park, with just our families standing beside us and becoming one. But the town got wind of it, and then everyone showed up, including my two brothers. They brought lawn chairs, presents, and potluck dishes. A buffet line was set up at the fire station, and no one cared if they ate off paper plates in 60-degree weather.

"It's the best surprise ever!" Ava shouts. She's holding my hand so that I don't trip over Finn's feet as I shuffle down the sidewalk.

The murmuring of people surrounds me as Finn brings us to a halt. "Are you ready?"

"I'm not sure. Your last surprise ended up with me doing an impromptu polar plunge in the lake," I tell him. Finn had rented a boat to take me on a romantic picnic to Dome Island, which is a small, forested swath of land in the middle of Lake George. The picnic was fabulous, but falling overboard—not so much.

Finn chuckles. "I promise this one is even better. Do you trust me?"

"I better. I married you."

"Show her already! The suspense is killing me!" someone shouts. "Do it on three!"

The crowd shouts, "One! Two! Three!"

Finn removes his hands, and my eyes slowly adjust to the light. I bring the tips of my fingers to my lips as my mouth forms a small "O." Eyes welling with tears, I turn and face the love of my life. "You bought me a bakery? How? When?"

Finn wraps his arms around me and puts his forehead to mine. "It wasn't just me, Bailey. The whole town pitched in to make this happen. Surprisingly, Daniel helped me order all the equipment you would need while Ella and Amanda helped design the layout. Bryce and a few other firefighters volunteered their time to build the cabinets, counters, and workspace."

I turn in Finn's arms and glance around the crowd, finding Daniel standing behind Amanda with his arms wrapped around her. Who knew that the two of them would find love with one another after a New Year's Eve kiss? "Thank you. Thank you all!"

"Does this mean we get free pastries and coffee?" Bryce asks, hopefully.

I laugh. "Firefighters, Police officers, and Vets will always get a special treat from Baileys and Buttercream!"

I walk over and touch the logo etched in the glass, running my fingers over every inch. "Can I get a tour?"

Finn entwines his fingers with mine and then brings my hand to his lips, kissing every knuckle with reverence. "It would be my absolute pleasure, milady."

When we enter the bakery, my eyes widen as big as the saucers that my pastries will be served on. Mia points to the corner where two wingback chairs sit and a sign over it that reads *Book Nook*. "That's my contribution because people need a special place to read. There's even a book exchange where people can swap books."

In between the two chairs is a corner tower full of books. "That's perfect and a brilliant idea!" I say, kissing the top of Mia's head.

I walk through the storefront and in the back, noting the top-of-the-line equipment and hand-carved wood counters. Once I'm done, my entire family waits for me as I absorb the magnitude of this gift. Wearing huge smiles, Ella and Micah lean against the counters, with Jonah, Isaac, and Ava standing in front of them. My parents frame the picture-perfect moment as Mia continues to chatter about all the amenities.

I hug my husband and kiss his cheek. "When I saw this storefront had been rented, my heart dropped because it was the perfect place to set up shop. How did you do this without me knowing about it?" I ask. "More importantly, how did you afford it, Finn? I would have seen the withdrawal in our bank account."

I had planned on renting the space as soon as the check cleared from the sale of the house. I had an offer in hand when the "Space for Rent" sign had been taken down.

Finn holds up a finger, gesturing for me to wait. He walks over to the front and waves someone inside. A few seconds later, Daniel enters with Amanda at his side. Finn slings an arm over Daniel's shoulder. "I can't take credit for the rental. It's all Daniel with that one."

Amanda beams at Daniel and then kisses his cheek before leaving him alone with us. Daniel swallows hard as he glances around the room. "I wanted to right a wrong," he says. "I couldn't buy the restaurant back for you, Bailey, but I could give you this. I used my half from the sale of the house to lease the space for you for the next three years. It was the least I could do, and I owed it to you and the girls."

Daniel has come a long way in the six months he's been home, and his relationship with our daughters has become closer than ever. He and Amanda have been coming to church, and it has been a miraculous turnaround for my ex. I hug Daniel. "Thank you. You didn't have to do this because I already forgave you. But I'm grateful that you did. At Christmas, you told me that you wanted to be a good man and a good father. You've succeeded, Daniel. I'm happy to call you a friend."

He embraces me back. "Thank you for that."

I step out of Daniel's hold and slide my arms around Finn's waist. I tell everyone that we'll be back in a minute and drag my husband behind me to the kitchen area.

Finn picks me up and sets me on the counter, nestling himself between my legs and caging me in with his arms. I don't hesitate to lace my fingers in his hair and pull his lips toward mine. As our mouths crash together and our tongues dance in harmony, I know that my place is here in his arms. After a few minutes of showing our appreciation for one another, Finn slows down and nips my lower lip. I always love it when he does that. "Was Ava right?" he asks.

"Right about what?"

He waves his hand around the kitchen and toward the front, where our family is still waiting for us. "Is this the best surprise ever?"

I tilt my head and smile at the enthusiasm in my husband's eyes. "It's a very close second."

Finn scrunches his nose. "What could be better than this?"

I pull out a small, wrapped box and hand it to him. "This." I watch as he unwraps the gift, and it takes him a moment to register what I'm giving him.

His eyes meet mine, and they're filled with tears. "You're right. This is so much better." He takes off toward the front of the store, waving the gift high above his head like a child who got their most wanted toy at Christmas. It's all I can do to keep up with him, but I'm too busy laughing as I push through the door that separates the kitchen from the lobby just as he shows off his present.

He whoops and hollers, holding the stick with two lines for everyone to see. "We're going to have a baby! Best gift ever!"

There is a round of congratulations for us both and a group hug that consists of a dozen people. Once the announcement is made outside, fire engine horns blare and the townies go wild. The mayor shouts, "I guess I'm going to have to change the town sign to read population 3,500 plus 1!"

Finn laughs and kisses me before addressing the crowd. "I'd hold off on that, Mayor, because I plan to make our family even bigger!"

## THE END

*The Sweet Christmas Series*

I hope you fell in love with Finn and Bailey.
I had so much fun writing their story!

Don't miss out on the rest of
**The *Sweet Christmas Kisses* Series!**

You can find all twelve standalone kisses-only
romance stories on Amazon here.

***Jingle Bells Rock and Roll*** by Evie Sterling
***A Doctor's Snowed In Christmas*** Wish by Daisy Flynn
***Love Rekindled at Evergreen Inn*** by Willa Lyons
***Stuck With My Christmas Crush*** by Francesca Spencer
***A Not So Merry Ex-Mas*** by Abby Greyson
***A Christmas Call of Duty*** by Ava Wakefield
***Finding Me In The Storm*** by Hazel Belle
***Snowbound With My Grumpy Ex*** by Lily Waters
***Sleighed By The Farmer's Daughter*** by Deanna Lilly
***Cabin Fever With My First Flame*** by Madison Love
***Faking It With My Bossy Ex*** by Leah Blair
***A Holly Jolly Mix Up*** by Bella Greene

Click here to start reading the rest of
The *Sweet Christmas Kisses* Series.
or scan

*Coming Soon!*

If you like this book, then you'll love what's in store.

**The Beanbaggers of Cornhole County: The Prequel**

Available on Amazon and Kindle Unlimited Here!

·▾ · ♥ · ♥ · ♥ ·▾·

**Four beanbags. Three nosy busybodies. Two hearts entwined, and one game that unites us all: Cornhole—where *board*-om doesn't exist and the unexpected can happen.**

### ***Josie***

Married for years and happily in love, Morgan and I trade in our city-slicker lifestyle after I'm diagnosed with the big, bad "C." It's not the end of the line. It's only the beginning.

Wanting peace and quiet, we move to a small town in the heart of Texas where the bovines outnumber the people 50 to 1, and chucking corn is considered a professional sport.

Embracing the Christmas spirit and needing something to do, I volunteer us to run the afterschool program. It turns out that I bit off more than I could chew.

Thankfully, I've got God, my husband, and the "Baggersville Biddies" on my side. The one thing I'm afraid I don't have is...

Time.

### ***Morgan***

A riding lawnmower, a suped-up truck, and a trunk full of cornhole boards might sound like the start of a joke, but it's my life.

Moving from the city to the country, I've traded in my tailored suit and shiny shoes for butt-hugging jeans and cowboy boots. I'll admit, it's a good look for me, and my wife agrees.

With a bat of her lashes, Josie wrangles me into building the backyard game as a fundraiser to help the community. After she ends up in the hospital, it's the community that comes to our aid.

I've never cared about getting presents before, but this time I ask for a gift that only God can give. Because what I really want more than anything is a Christmas miracle. My Josie.

·♥·♥·♥·♥·♥·

**\*\*\* *The Beanbaggers of Cornhole County*** is a Christian, Sweet, Kisses-only romance series prequel that's sure to make you smile and is free from profanity, promiscuity, or cheating by the protagonists in the story. It's an introduction to the main characters in the follow-on books.

**<u>TRIGGER WARNING</u>**: (Note from the author) Although there is plenty of humor and banter in this story, this book touches on the topic of cancer, which is no laughing matter (The humor found within the pages is *not* related to this sensitive topic). If this subject is a trigger for you, please do not read this prequel. It is never my intention to harm or hurt anyone, but this story is near and dear to my heart. I do my best to treat the subject matter with the utmost respect, care, and consideration. And like all my books, it ends with a HEA.

# Excerpt from The Beanbaggers of Cornhole County

## Chapter 1 - Josie

"Tell me again why you wanted to move to a small town in the middle of Nowheresville, Texas?" my husband, Morgan, asks as he shuts off the Cub Cadet riding lawn mower he purchased shortly after we arrived. Our penthouse living and city-slicker lifestyle never warranted the need for such a machine, but after a lengthy tutorial from Meril at the feed store, it's become my husband's pride and joy.

"It's not 'Nowheresville,' Honey. The town is called Baggersville, and it's in the heart of Cornhole County. Who wouldn't want to move here with a name like that? Besides, I thought the lack of an "L" and an extra 'R' in our words sounded like an adventure," I tease. "I love having soup in a *bread bow* and doing laundry with our new *warshing* machine."

Removing the ball cap from his head and shaking out the excess sweat, he gives me one of his dazzling smiles that always makes my heart pitter-patter and skip a beat. "Don't go forgettin' the lack of a 'G' at the end of a verb. It's like we're speakin' another language livin' down here. Next thing ya' know, we'll be greetin' people with the phrase, 'Hi, Y'all!'"

I shrug. "'Y'all' has got to be one of the friendliest words on the planet, and I adore it almost as much as I adore you."

Morgan saunters up the steps, his body coated in dewy moisture and grass clippings from mowing our ten acres of lawn. He prowls toward me like a lion on the hunt and slides his arms around my body, pulling me close—not to shower me with kisses but to rub his grime all over me. "You love me a lot, so that's saying something."

I do love my husband more than life itself. Two years ago and out of nowhere, I collapsed in our apartment while my husband was at work. As a CEO, he spent more time at the office than at home, but it all changed after that fateful day. I was diagnosed with an inoperable brain tumor that left me spending the next couple of years going through rigorous chemotherapy treatments that did nothing more than shrink the tumor. He never left my side.

After a lengthy and heartfelt discussion that left us both reeling and in tears, we decided as a team that I would live out the last few years of my life the best way possible. The chemotherapy treatments stopped, and we sold our penthouse apartment to move to Baggersville, where the air is as fresh as the cow patties, and the bovines outnumber the people fifty to one.

I try my best to push my husband away, but he tightens his grip and rubs his body against me. Laughing, he says, "I think it's only fair that if I have to get dirty, then so do you, Josie."

"You're just looking forward to the cleanup," I wink.

Morgan sweeps me off my feet and touches his lips toward mine. "Yes. Yes, I am."

A few hours later, thoroughly clean and content, Morgan and I sit around the dining room table. He's managing our portfolio on his laptop while I peruse the local paper for a part-time job. His eyes peer at me over the top of his screen. "Josie, why are you looking for a job? I thought we moved out here so you can rest."

I wad up the four-page, small-town newspaper that has the headline, *Baggersville Bessie Boasts Another Blue Ribbon at Cornhole County Fair*, and throw it at my husband's head. "I'm bored, Morgan. You got to trade in your pressed suit and shiny shoes for butt-hugging jeans and cowboy boots. You get to ride around on the spiffy mower, work in your woodshop, and day trade. Not to mention, you get to look sexy doing it. I know I'm supposed to take it easy, but that doesn't mean not doing anything at all. And before you say it, burning through two e-readers doesn't count. Although, I'll admit that I'm proud of that accomplishment."

Morgan chuckles. "You should be. Have you given any thought to my suggestion of writing? You always had a creative spark swirling around in that beautiful head of yours."

I rub my short hair, which is finally starting to grow back. "My creativity is limited to latte art and drink concoctions, not creating story arcs and weaving plot lines," I sigh. "I miss my coffee shop and interacting with the customers."

He taps a few buttons on his keyboard and then closes his laptop to focus on me. Morgan reaches across the table and laces his fingers with mine, using the pad of his thumb to rub small circles on my hand. "Josie, Baby, what is it that you want to do? There aren't a whole lot of job opportunities in town."

My husband is right about that. The town has less than 2,000 people, and I can walk from end to end in under ten minutes. There's a gas station, diner, small library, and church. There's also a small grocery store for basic necessities, but otherwise, we have to drive 45 minutes to the nearest town that has a Walmart or Costco. The church is the hub of the town unless there is a high school football game going on, which is a huge draw here in Texas. But then again, everything in Texas is huge.

"I don't know, that's why I was looking," I tell him. "I just need something that gets me out of the house, even if it's only for a couple of hours a few days a week. I don't need a nine-to-five or anything, but I do want to feel useful."

"I can build you a coffee shop, and then you can do your thing," Morgan says. With billions of dollars in our account, it wouldn't be a hardship.

I give his idea careful consideration before shaking my head and tapping my temple. "Maybe if my little friend miraculously disappears forever, then it might be worth pursuing. Besides, people around here expect their coffee to come from a plastic tub, and anything other than that is considered *hoity toity* or *highfalutin*."

I drop my voice to mimic Meril when we first moved here and asked him where we could grab a bite to eat, "This town ain't the kind of place where people come for fancy dinin' or anythin' snazzy. We got Lucy's Diner, where you can get the best steaks in Texas and a slice of fresh peach pie. Lucy can doodad it up for you with a scoop of homemade vanilla bean ice cream, though."

Morgan laughs. "I see your point. How about we go into town and split one of those steaks at Lucy's and see what kind of gossip is going on at the local watering hole? If anyone knows of a job that isn't listed in the *Pennysaver*, it would be the town folk at the diner."

We often split the steak at Lucy's because it's ginormous and takes up half the table. "Sounds like a plan to me. I didn't have anything defrosted for dinner. Let me grab my purse and hair. Then I'll be ready to go."

"Josie, you are beautiful just the way you are."

I kiss his cheek. "Thank you, but I don't wear the wig because I'm embarrassed. I simply don't want the questions or the pity. I just want a nice night out with my husband. When the people in this town start calling us by our names and not 'The New Yorkers,' I'll consider letting them in. Deal? You love making deals."

He nods and reaches for my sweater hanging on the coat hook by the front door. "Deal."

I head toward our bedroom and put the realistic-looking wig made of chestnut brown human hair on my head, taking a little extra time to tame a few of the loose strands going wild. I grab my purse and skip toward the front of the house, where Morgan holds up my sweater.

"It's hard to believe it's the first day of December when it's still 60 degrees outside—at night, no less," I say as I slip my arms into the sleeves. "The chances of having a white Christmas seem to be slipping further and further away."

"That ship sailed the moment the dart hit the town of Baggersville, Babe. Although, Texas has been known to get snow on occasion, so you might get lucky."

I scoff. "I did not throw a dart at a map to choose this location! It was a well-thought-out decision where the pros and cons were weighed."

"Josie, you may not have thrown a dart, but picking a name out of a hat does not equate to being well-thought-out."

Morgan walks me to the Lexus LS 500 parked in the driveway, his hand never leaving the small of my back. He loves to tease me, but he knows that I spent weeks hunting for the perfect home. I narrowed it down to five in Texas—where part of my family now lives. My older sister lives three hours away in Dallas, which is close enough for her to visit but far enough that she can't go all 'mother hen' on me.

I slide into the plush leather seats, running my fingers over the supple material. When Morgan gets behind the wheel, I turn to him and wipe a fake tear from my eye. "It's going to be a sad day when you have to trade this beauty in for a truck."

His eyebrows reach his hairline. "Why on earth do I have to get rid of my car?"

I hold in my laugh because I would never ask Morgan to get rid of his car, but I continue to mess with him just for fun. I gesture to the pastures surrounding our home. "It doesn't really go with the motif. A suped-up pickup truck would be more appropriate to the area. What if you need to haul fertilizer for my garden or a load of lumber for your workshop? What if you get stuck in the mud and there's no one around to help you?" Now that I think about it, a truck would be a great addition.

"A few bags of fertilizer do not require a truck, Josie. As of now, my projects in the shop are limited to small hope chests and salad bowls, not armoires or dining room tables that can seat a dozen people. I think we're good, but the lumber shop delivers if I decide to up my game. As far as getting stuck, then I probably shouldn't have been driving on non-paved roads to begin with," he says, taking me far more seriously than I intended.

"But you would look so sexy in a truck!" I tease, sort of. Morgan would look sexy in anything he drives. The way his corded muscles flex when he grips the wheel always gets heart revving.

He narrows his gaze. "I look sexy now, Josie. That's one of the many reasons you married me."

I bob my head. "It's one reason, but far from being the most important one."

He places his large palm on my thigh and gives me a smoldering look. "And what reason tops the list?"

I run my fingers through his hair that's getting a little long and curling at the edges. "Because you make me smile."

*Also By Madison Love*

*Sweet Romantic Suspense*

## **The Just4You Matchmaker Series**
Matchmaking the Protector – Prequel
Matchmaking the Undercover Agent – Book 1
Matchmaking the Grumpy Doctor – Book 2
Matchmaking the Firefighter – Book 3

·♥·♥·♥·♥·♥·

## **Shining Knight Protector Series**
Valiant
Honor Bound
Worthy
Resolute
Daring
Fearless

Made in the USA
Columbia, SC
16 January 2025